THE SUPERHERO'S TEST

The Superhero's Son #1
Lucas Flint

An Annulus Publishing Book

Annulus Publishing, Cherokee, Texas, 2016

Published by Secret Identity Books. An imprint of Annulus Publishing.

Copyright © Lucas Flint 2016. All rights reserved.

Contact: luke@lucasflint.com

Cover design by Damonza (https://damonza.com/)

ISBN-13: 978-0692733240

ISBN-10: 0692733248

CHAPTER ONE

MY MOM ALWAYS SAID that I have a strong arm, but I always thought it was just one of those things that moms say to their sons … at least before I punched the local school bully through the cafeteria wall with one blow after I lost my temper.

Maybe I should back up a bit and explain how I got to this point. Maybe something happened along the way that gave me my superpowers, that would explain how I got here. Dad always says that, whenever you find yourself in a mess of a situation, retracing your steps can help you figure out how you got into it in the first place, so I'll do that.

My name is Kevin Jake Jason and I am seventeen-years-old and an only child. Earlier today, I started my first day at my new school, John Smith High School, located in Silvers, Texas, which is a pretty small, obscure town that no one seems to know about. My parents and I moved here from New York City during the summer because it's supposed to be cheaper, but I think Dad just wanted to get as far away from my mother's parents as possible. I didn't really want to move, but I decided to roll with it because I've always liked cowboys and Westerns and thought Texas girls might be cuter than New York girls (or that's what one of my New York friends who has family in Texas told me, anyway).

Anyway, like I said, today was my first day at my new school. It was a lot smaller than my old school back in New York; just a few hundred students versus a few thousand. Even so, I still felt awkward, because I was the new kid and I literally didn't know anybody. It was pretty easy for me to figure out who the jocks were, who the popular girls were, who the nerds were, and so on, but I still found it hard to approach anyone, and I'm no introvert— Dad was, though, but that's because my Dad is a software developer.

But it wasn't all bad. I got through the first period okay without running into any real harassment or bullying. Most of the students and faculty were a lot nicer and friendlier than the students and faculty back in my old school in New York, but it just seemed like a sort of obligatory friendliness, like Texans were supposed to be polite to strangers. And that was what I was, really, because like I said, I didn't know anyone and no one knew me.

That was why I dreaded lunchtime. Back in my old school, I always sat with my friends David and James, but David and James were still in New York. I was facing the very real possibility of sitting by myself at lunch today, which was something I hadn't experienced since first grade.

So when the bell rang and the students went to lunch, I found myself briefly debating whether or not I should just skip it. But I was so hungry that I went to lunch anyway, deciding that I could suffer a little embarrassment if it meant getting something to eat.

And when I got to the cafeteria, I quickly discovered that pretty much everyone—including the nerds—had their own cliques that they ate with. With my tray in hand, I stood in the cafeteria, looking for an open table I could sit at, but it seemed like every table was full and no one looked eager to invite the new kid to sit with them. No one even seemed to notice me, although a few of the popular girls sitting at a nearby table kept glancing at me like they were afraid that a loser like me would try to sit next to them. Not that I thought I was a loser, but I knew they probably did, based on the way they looked at me.

Every table, that is, except for the one in the upper right corner of the room. A black guy sat there by himself, seemingly without any friends of his own. Of course, he might have just been waiting for his friends, but he didn't really look like he belonged to any of the other groups. He wore a long-sleeved shirt and baggy jeans, but he didn't look much like a jock or a nerd. I noticed he had some kind of necklace tucked into his shirt, which made it impossible to see what was attached.

But the guy didn't look very judgmental, so I made my way across the noisy cafeteria to him. I accidentally walked into a big guy with dark skin and blond hair, who glared at me as I walked around him apologizing for not watching where I was going. He didn't follow me, but I felt like his eyes never stopped following me as I walked over to the guy sitting by himself at that table in the corner of the cafeteria.

As I approached the table, the black guy looked up at me. He seemed surprised that someone was coming up to his table, which confirmed to me that he always sat by himself.

"Hi," I said, stopping at the table. "Anyone sitting here?"

The guy shook his head. "No, it's open. Sit where you like."

"Thanks," I said. I sat down opposite him and put down my tray on the table between us. "By the way, my name is Kevin

Jason. What's yours?"

"Malcolm Rayner," said the guy. "You're the new kid, right?"

"How did you know?" I said.

"Because I've never seen you before," said Malcolm. "I know pretty much everyone in this school, so when I saw someone I didn't know, I thought you were new."

"You know everyone?" I said as I sipped from my water bottle. "You must be pretty popular, then."

Malcolm chuckled. "Popular? Nah. It's just a small school, so you get to know everyone pretty quickly even if you don't have any friends."

"Oh," I said. My earlier suspicion was correct, but I decided to change the subject because Malcolm didn't sound like he really liked talking about his popularity—or lack thereof—in the school. "So, uh, do you usually sit by yourself?"

Malcolm shrugged. "Eh, sometimes. But it's not a big deal to me. I'm used to it. Anyway, where are you from?"

"New York," I said. "New York City, that is."

"Really?" said Malcolm in surprise. "What are you doing all the way out here?"

I shrugged as I took a bite out of my tuna sandwich. "My parents decided to move down here because it's cheaper than living back there."

"Cool," said Malcolm. "I've never been to New York City before." He leaned forward, an interested look on his face. "Have you been to Hero Island? I heard the Neohero Alliance let's normal people go on tours around the place for a fee."

I figured he was going to ask me about that place once I told him I was from NYC, mostly because it seemed like everyone who didn't live in NYC wanted to know all about the main base and headquarters of the largest superhero organization in the world. It was located on Hero Island, an artificial island created by the neohero Mr. Miner twenty-five years ago to give the Neohero Alliance a base of operations. I didn't mind talking about it, but it got kind of annoying to be asked about it every time I told someone I was from NYC.

So I said, "No, but I've seen it. My parents never let me visit it. They thought it wasn't safe."

"Not safe?" said Malcolm in disbelief. "But Hero Island has a bunch of powerful neoheroes on it, right? I mean, Omega Man himself lives there and he's the most powerful neohero on the planet. It seems to me like the safest place in the world, if you ask me. I wish I could go there myself some day. It would be awesome."

"Some of my friends back home visited it," I said. "But they said it was kind of boring because they just got to see the Neohero Alliance Museum and a few places deemed safe for tourists. They didn't get to see the training facilities or the places where they store the weapons they take from defeated supervillains or anything like that."

"They probably only let real members of the NHA explore the rest of the base," said Malcolm. He sighed. "It would be awesome to get to meet Omega Man himself."

I nodded. Omega Man was one of the first neoheroes and the most well-known and beloved. I had only ever seen him on Internet videos and pictures, but I knew he lived in NYC and was from the city. I had never actually met him, but Dad said he met Omega Man once, a long time ago. Dad never told me much about that meeting, though, except that it was brief.

"So what's this school like?" I said as I took another bite of my sandwich. "Anything crazy ever happen here?"

Malcolm shook his head. "Nah. It's pretty quiet most of the time. Even the pranksters don't usually do anything *that* crazy. Not that I'm complaining, though."

That was disappointing to hear. Back in my school in New York, there was an entire subculture of kids who pranked students and school faculty alike. Every year, these kids would get together to make the biggest and wildest prank of the year, known as the Big One, which was always supposed to top last year's Big One. Granted, sometimes they got out of control—the last Big One resulted in the entire school evacuating and several members of the NHA arriving under the belief that the supervillain Judgment had taken over the school—but I always looked forward to them and even helped organize a few, but always on the periphery, because I wasn't considered one of the pranksters even though I always enjoyed a good prank myself.

Then I noticed Malcolm's necklace again and said, "What's that on your neck?"

Malcolm looked down at his necklace tucked into his shirt. "Oh, this? Er, it's nothing. Just something my grandma gave me."

"Can I see it?" I said.

Malcolm hesitated, like he wasn't sure whether to say yes or no, but before he could answer, a tray slammed down on the table next to me and a second later a girl of about my age sat down next to me. Her sudden appearance next to me made me scoot to the side involuntarily, but the girl didn't even seem to notice me because she was looking at something on her smartphone.

THE SUPERHERO'S TEST

The girl was kind of cute. She had blonde hair and blue eyes, though her yellow shirt was rather plain. She wore jeans and had a belt with rhinestones on it, which were hard to look at directly because they reflected the light from the ceiling so much. Her smartphone had a rhinestone case, though it looked a little beat up like she didn't take very good care of it.

"Hey, Tara," said Malcolm, though he didn't sound very excited to see her. "What's up?"

"Hey, Malcolm," said Tara, still without looking at Malcolm or me, her focus on her smartphone.

That was all Tara said. She still didn't look at me, which made me think that she either didn't think I was worth her notice or she was just too absorbed by her smartphone to pay attention to me. Regardless, I felt too nervous to say anything, and it wasn't just because I was the new kid in school, either.

"Oh, uh, Kevin, this is Tara Reynolds," said Malcolm, gesturing at her. "Tara, this is the new kid, Kevin Jason."

Tara looked up from her phone just long enough to look at me through her glasses before returning her attention to the device in her hand. "Nice meeting you, Kevin."

"Uh, nice meeting you, too," I said. I looked at Malcolm. "Is she your friend?"

"We know each other," said Malcolm. "We, er, don't really have any other friends."

"We just sort of hang out together because no one else likes us," said Tara, again without looking at me or Malcolm. Her response surprised me, because I hadn't realized that she had been listening.

That was when I realized that I was hanging out with the

freaks. I mean, not that I hated Malcolm or Tara, but I hadn't realized that they were clearly on the bottom of the John Smith High School pecking order until this moment. Just my luck, I suppose, that I, the new kid, would end up eating lunch with the two least popular kids in the school, which probably meant that the rest of the school would always associate me with these two even if I stopped hanging out with them.

While that realization sank in, Malcolm looked at Tara again and said, "Oh, hey, Tara, did you know that Kevin is from New York? We were just talking about Hero Island and how awesome it would be to go there."

Tara suddenly froze. I didn't know her very well, but even I could tell that Malcolm had accidentally stepped on an emotional minefield. I fully expected her to throw her smartphone at Malcolm or maybe just throw him out the window.

But then Tara relaxed and said, in a tense voice, "I wouldn't want to go there. Those neoheroes aren't anything special."

"What?" said Malcolm. "Oh, come on, Tara. Omega Man is awesome. And the Midnight Menace, too."

"All they do is cause destruction and get innocent people caught in the crossfire of their dangerous battles," said Tara, still without looking at either of us. "Personally, I think we'd be better off without them."

Frankly, I was stunned by her excessive negativity toward neoheroes. I've always known that there were some people who hate anyone with super powers, whether they do good things or bad with those powers, but I didn't really encounter too many of those people back in New York. I'm not as big a neohero fan as Malcolm, but I liked them a lot and always thought it would be cool to become a neohero myself.

But I could tell that Tara had other reasons for disliking neoheroes. She didn't scream or shout, but I could tell that she must have been letting some of her personal experiences with them affect her. I considered asking her, but then realized that that would be like sticking your hand into a meat grinder just to see what happens.

Despite Tara's negativity, I still thought she was cute and was going to ask her out before a harsh voice behind me shouted, "Hey, new kid!"

Uh oh. I knew *that* tone. It was the sort of tone that all bullies used whenever they addressed their next victims. Or, at least, that was the tone bullies back in my old school used, which almost made me think that one of my old bullies somehow traveled all the way from New York to Texas just to pick up where we left off.

Nonetheless, I looked over my shoulder and saw a large guy with tanned skin and blond hair—the same guy I bumped into earlier—walking toward our table. He was taller and larger than me, wearing an old leather jacket that just made him look even more intimidating. He looked vaguely Mexican, but he looked like he might have had some other race in him, too, though I wasn't sure which.

"Uh oh," said Malcolm with a gulp. "That's Robert Candle, the local bully."

"Why does he seem angry with me?" I said as I tried to calculate how much time I had before he arrived.

"It's a John Smith High School tradition," said Tara. "Robert always 'greets' the new kids, usually by stuffing them into a locker or making them give him their lunch."

"Or both," said Malcolm.

I hated dealing with bullies. It wasn't that I was a coward or small and weak; I was actually really strong. It's just that I'm bad at fighting and I've gotten in trouble at my old school for defending myself from the bullies there. I always found it easier to just go along with whatever the bullies demanded of me than make a scene and get in trouble with the school administration.

But there wasn't any running or making peace now. Robert looked like he was pissed, so I stood and tried to look as tough as I could, mostly because I knew that some bullies would leave you alone if you looked as tough as or tougher than them.

Robert, apparently, wasn't one of those kinds of bullies, because when he reached our table, he looked completely unimpressed by my tough guy act. He was taller than me, almost towering over me, though it was probably just his angry demeanor that made me think he was so much bigger than me.

Still, I did not cower before him. I just said, "Hi, Robert. What's the problem?"

"I'm not going to ask how you know my name, loser," said Robert. He poked me in the chest with one of his large fingers. "But don't play dumb with me. You know what you did."

"No, I don't," I said. Robert's tone was annoying me, but I tried to keep my cool. "I really don't."

"You bumped into me back there," said Robert, jerking his thumb over his shoulder. "Remember? It was just five minutes ago."

I nodded, albeit slowly. "Yes, I do, but I apologized."

"I don't care," said Robert. "I don't accept apologies. I think you were intentionally trying to piss me off."

"Why?" I said. "I just got here. I don't even know you. Why would I go out of my way to make you angry?"

"I don't know why, but I think you did," said Robert. "But I'm willing to overlook it if you would give me your lunch every day for the next week."

"What?" I said, not bothering to hide the indignation in my voice. "You want me to give you my lunch for all of next week?"

"Yes," said Robert. "If you do that, I might be able to overlook such stupid behavior from a kid as green as yourself."

I raised an eyebrow. "A kid? We're probably the same age."

"Shut up," Robert growled. "I know what I said."

I didn't think he did, but I decided not to say anything that could escalate the situation, although that was hard because my temper was starting to rise. Mom always told me that I should control my temper, but it was always hard to do whenever I was talking with a bully like Robert.

Still, I managed to say, in a calm voice, "What will happen if I say no?"

"Then I'll just beat you up and take your lunch," said Robert. "Every day for the next week, I'll give you a progressively worse beating and then take your lunch."

"What the hell?" I said. I stopped myself quickly, taking a few deep breaths to control my temper, and then said more calmly, "What? That's not a fair choice. Either way, you get my lunch every day for the next week."

Robert smiled, a psychotic smile that I wanted to wipe off his face. "And? Why should I care? You're the new kid around here. That means you don't get a choice about what we choose to put you through."

My hands balled into fists, but I shoved them into my hoodie. But that did nothing to cool the anger boiling within me.

I looked at Malcolm and Tara. "Guys, is he for real? Tell me this is some kind of elaborate prank."

Unfortunately, Malcolm and Tara seemed to be trying to turn invisible, because Malcolm was looking at his food as if it was the most interesting thing in the world, while Tara had brought her smartphone even closer to her face. I would have considered this a betrayal, but neither of them were really my friends, so maybe I should have seen that coming.

Regardless, I looked at Robert again, who was still smirking at me. He put his hands on his hips and said, "All right, new kid, what will it be? Give up your lunch for a week or receive a beating from me and still lose your lunch for a week?"

My hands shook. I was starting to fantasize about knocking Robert out in one blow, but I kept myself from doing something I'd regret.

But neither was I going to stand here and take it. So I said, "Sorry, Robert, but looks like you're going to have to get your own lunch this—"

I didn't even see it coming. Robert's fist smashed into my abdomen, knocking the air out of me. I gasped in pain and fell down onto my seat at the table, causing Malcolm and even Tara to look at me in surprise.

Wrapping my hands over my stomach, I looked up at Robert, who was now holding his fist up like he was going to mash my head in.

"You just *had* to make things difficult, didn't you, new kid?"

said Robert. He snorted. "Oh, well. It's been a while since I've gotten to beat a new kid. Most new kids don't have the balls to say no to me."

Damn, Robert hit *hard*. He really was as strong as he looked. Yet I didn't let the pain make me cower. Instead, it made me angrier than ever. My anger rose within me like a geyser and I was just about ready to blow.

Robert swung another fist at me, this time aiming for my head, but I caught his fist with my hand. I expected it to be hard to hold back, but to my surprise, I held back Robert's fist with ease.

"What?" said Robert. He sounded genuinely shocked, like he was incapable of understanding what was happening. "How did you do that?"

I wasn't sure how, because I had never done that before. But I didn't question it. I just stood up, forcing Robert's fist back as I did so. Anger continued to flow through my veins and I wasn't going to be calm anymore.

Robert seemed to get over his shock, because he pulled back his other fist and threw it at me. But I dodged it easily and responded with a punch of my own, aiming for his chest, which was unprotected and a big target.

When my fist collided with Robert's chest, Robert literally went flying. He flew backwards through the air, across the entire length of the cafeteria, screaming loudly and drawing the attention of everyone in the cafeteria. Hundreds of pairs of eyes followed Robert as he flew, until he smashed straight through the cafeteria wall and stopped screaming.

I stood there, blinking in disbelief. I looked down at my own fist, which looked no worse the wear for having punched a big guy like Robert all the way across the cafeteria. The only thing I noticed was how strong I felt, but I was too shocked to pay attention even to that.

Then I looked at Malcolm and Tara. Malcolm was staring at me like I had grown a set of wings and flew away, while Tara had actually dropped her smartphone onto the table and stared at me with the same shock as Malcolm.

That was when I felt people looking at me and looked back at the rest of the cafeteria. Everyone in the cafeteria was looking directly at me, wearing expressions as the ones Malcolm and Tara wore. I probably looked the same, but I didn't have a mirror so I couldn't see my face.

All I knew was that I had possibly just murdered another kid … and I hadn't even known I could do it.

CHAPTER TWO

W HY WASN'T ANYONE TALKING? I hated it when things got silent like this. Everyone was staring at me. Everyone was looking at me like I was some kind of freak. Even the lunch lady behind the cafeteria counter was staring at me soundlessly, holding a spoon full of grub halfway in the air. The only sound was the sound of bits of plaster and plywood falling onto the floor from the Robert Candle-shaped hole in the wall on the other side of the room.

Feeling hot around the collar, I looked at Malcolm and Tara. They seemed to have completely lost the ability to talk. I thought that their brains probably hadn't caught up with the reality of what they just saw yet.

Then, all of a sudden, Robert groaned from behind the hole in the wall. Like a spell, the entire classroom suddenly burst into loud screaming and shouting. The other kids started pointed and shouting at me, like I was some kind of monster, while a couple of teachers ran into the cafeteria. It was Mr. Randal, the English teacher, and Miss Norman, the History teacher, who were now trying to figure out what happened, but there was too much screaming and shouting for them to make sense of what happened.

Again, I looked back at Malcolm and Tara. I said, raising my voice to be heard over the screams echoing in the cafeteria, "I don't know what happened! You have to believe me!"

But Malcolm and Tara were now looking at me with the same fear that the other kids had. Tara was even scooting away from me on the bench, while Malcolm looked like he was trying to figure out if he should run or try to confront me. Although neither of them were really my friends, I still felt awful about frightening them with powers I didn't even know I had.

Then I heard a loud voice shout, "Kevin Jason!" and I looked and saw a large, balding middle-aged man in a suit walking up to me. I recognized him as Principal Thomas, the principal of John Smith High School, who I hadn't actually met until today. I wasn't sure where he came from, but it didn't matter because he was clearly pissed.

"What is the meaning of this?" said Principal Thomas as he approached me. "I heard you punched a student through the walls. Explain yourself!"

I didn't know what to say. I held up my hands to show that I didn't mean any harm, but Principal Thomas just stepped backwards like he was afraid that I would punch him, too.

"I-I-I'm not sure," I said, stuttering more than I had ever stuttered in my life. "I—"

"I want no excuses," Principal Thomas interrupted me. He poked me in the chest with one meaty finger. "I am going to tell the police and your parents about this and will get to the bottom of this nonsense no matter what. I will not be having students in my school punching each other through the walls with powers they have not previously disclosed. Do you understand me, young man?"

THE SUPERHERO'S TEST

My temper flared again, because Principal Thomas was acting like I had intentionally hidden these powers from everyone, even though I was just as surprised by my super strength as anyone. I was almost tempted to punch him out, but I restrained my anger, though just barely.

"He understands you perfectly, Principal Thomas," said a slightly muffled, calm voice that seemed strangely familiar to me, but which I was too upset to place. "He just doesn't know his own strength is all."

I looked over to the corner of the cafeteria, where the voice had come from, and was surprised to see someone standing there. He was a tall man, about as tall as me, and wore a white lab coat and a strange-looking helmet with a visor that completely covered his face. He wore metal gauntlets that had touch screen displays and tons of buttons on them that I didn't understand at all. He was not the kind of person you'd expect to see in a small town Texas high school cafeteria, to say the least.

The man's appearance must have been noticed by everyone, because all of the screaming and shouting and crying in the cafeteria suddenly went silent. I looked back at the other students and faculty and saw that everyone was now staring at the newcomer, though with more confusion than fear.

Only Principal Thomas seemed to get over his confusion long enough to sputter, "Wh-Who are you?"

"Someone who is technically supposed to be in retirement," said the masked man as he walked up to my table, seemingly not bothered by all of the shocked and confused looks from everyone else.

"How did you get into the school without my knowledge?"

said Principal Thomas. "I don't remember being told that we were having a guest today."

"That's because you have incredibly poor security," said the masked man as he stopped next to me, again ignoring all the stares from everyone else. "If John Smith High School hadn't had such an excellence academic reputation, I'd rethink sending my son here."

"Huh?" said Principal Thomas. He genuinely seemed at a loss for words, like he wasn't sure whether to take the masked man's words as a compliment or an insult.

But there was something about the masked man's way of speaking that seemed familiar to me. I looked at him, but his mask and costume covered his body from head to toe, making it impossible for me to identify him. All I could tell was that he was obviously a neohero of some kind, but I just wasn't sure who.

Then Malcolm gasped and said, "Oh my gosh! You're Genius, right?"

The masked man looked at Malcolm, but he seemed more impressed than annoyed. "You recognize me?"

"Yeah!" said Malcolm. "I'm a big neohero fan and I know about almost every neohero in the world. You're one of the Four Founders of the Neohero Alliance, after all."

I vaguely recalled hearing about a neohero named Genius once, but I had never met him and didn't know much about him except that he was one of the first neoheroes. But I remembered hearing that he retired from crime-fighting, although no one knew what he was doing now due to keeping his secret identity, well, a secret.

"Well, that is quite flattering," said Genius. "But I am afraid I am going to have to erase this little meeting of ours from your memory. This is not a good way for a new neohero to debut to the world."

"What—" I said, before Genius pulled out a pair of dark shades and slammed them over my eyes, almost pushing me over because he hit me so hard.

Then, before anyone else could say anything, Genius raised one of his gauntlets, pressed a button on it, and a huge, blinding white flash exploded from the gauntlet. It covered the entire room, totally enveloping everyone before anyone could react. I now understood why Genius had slammed these shades on my eyes; they protected my vision, but now I was worried that everyone else would be struck blind by the explosion.

When the light faded, everyone was still staring at us, but now they looked completely dumbfounded. Their stares were blank. They almost looked like zombies. I half-expected Principal Thomas to raise his hands and start going around saying, "Brains! Brains!"

Genius lowered his gauntlet and said to the room, "You did not see Kevin Jason punch Robert Candle through the wall of the cafeteria. Instead, Robert had brought a homemade air bomb with him that accidentally exploded and sent him flying through the cafeteria wall. Kevin had nothing to do with it."

I was no Einstein, but even I could see through that blatant lie. It wasn't even a very good lie; I mean, there weren't any remains of the air bomb, after all.

But I guess I must have been the smartest person in the school, because the students, faculty, and Principal Thomas all nodded in agreement. Principal Thomas even repeated Genius's warning word by word, as if he was practicing it.

"All right," said Genius. He paused, and then added, "Oh, and Kevin Jason suffered from food poisoning due to your bad cafeteria food and had to go home early. He will be back in school tomorrow, so you do not need to follow up on him or call either of his parents about his whereabouts."

"Of course," said Principal Thomas, who sounded very absentminded. "Yes, yes, I understand. Our food really is terrible, but it's because our funding keeps getting slashed and we have to buy low quality food."

"I don't care," said Genius. He grabbed my arm suddenly and said, "All right, Kevin, let's go."

Before I could ask where we were going, Genius turned a dial on his utility belt and the cafeteria vanished around me in an instant.

A second later, I found myself standing in the living room of our new house. I recognized it because there were a few boxes containing some of our unpacked belongings in one corner, in addition to the distinctive red carpet that looked old but which my Dad insisted was cool. A picture of my family—me, my Dad, and my Mom—stood on the fireplace mantle, although it was the only family picture out because we were still searching for the others, which had somehow gotten lost in the move.

But that didn't matter, because I had just been kidnapped by a legendary superhero who was supposed to be in retirement. I looked to my right and saw Genius standing there, still holding my arm, which I yanked out of his hand as soon as my senses returned to me.

"What the hell was that about?" I said, removing the shades

from my eyes. I looked around the living room. "Is this really my house? Because if you kidnapped me, you did a bad job of it."

Genius looked like he was about to talk, but then I heard some movement from the kitchen and in the next instant Mom stood in the doorway in her apron, her red hair tied back behind her head and her green eyes wide in surprise. She held a long spoon in her hand, which she seemed to have been washing before coming in here, based on the way it dripped.

"Kevin?" said Mom in surprise. "What are you doing home from school so early?"

"Um—" I said, but it was Genius who spoke.

"He punched a bully through the wall of the cafeteria and I got him out before he landed in real big trouble," said Genius, his tone as calm as if this sort of thing happened every day.

"What?" said Mom. She looked at Genius and frowned. "What are you doing in that suit?"

Mom's tone was strange. It wasn't disapproving, exactly, but it wasn't exactly thrilled, either. It sounded almost like she already knew the answer to the question, but was asking it anyway because it was part of their routine.

"Because if I didn't, then everyone would know my secret identity," said Genius. "Besides, I can't use most of my gadgets without the suit."

"I thought you had put the suit away," said Mom. "I thought you were done with superhero stuff."

"Yes, but I had to step in just this once because if I hadn't, our son would have gotten into more trouble than teenage boys usually get into," said Genius.

I blinked. "Wait. *Our* son? You're not my Dad. I don't even know who you are." I looked at Mom in horror. "Did you cheat on Dad with Genius?"

"No, no, no," said Genius, shaking his head quickly. "I understand you're confused, so let me show you my real identity."

Genius put his hands on his helmet and lifted his helmet off of his head. Once it was off, I could now see Genius's face. I was shocked by what I saw.

The man standing in the Genius costume had the same brown hair and blue eyes that I did. We were almost identical in appearance, except he looked older and had streaks of gray through his hair. His eyes were more piercing than mine, too, a familiar look I had grown up experiencing, like he was constantly analyzing my every move and emotion.

"Dad?" I said in pure shock. "Is that you?"

Dad nodded, although he didn't smile. "Yes. And I have a lot of explaining to do, so let's sit down on the couch and have a talk we should have had a long time ago."

CHAPTER THREE

SITTING DOWN ON THE couch with Dad was a pretty normal thing most of the time. Usually, I'd be watching sports or something else on TV, while he'd be reading a book or one of his favorite news sites on his tablet. We never talked much, but it always felt normal to me.

But when I sat down with Dad on the couch now and put my shades on my lap, it felt strange. Dad was still in his Genius costume, which I was trying to tell myself was some kind of Halloween costume and that this was all some kind of strange prank or maybe even performance art before I remembered that Dad was a total introvert and hated doing anything that would draw attention to himself if he could avoid it.

Dad, however, didn't seem uncomfortable about this. He just sat down on the right end of the couch, where he usually sat, with his Genius helmet in his lap. I half-expected him to pull out his tablet or grab a book and start reading, but he just folded his hands over his helmet and looked at me like we were about to have a normal father-son conversation.

Mom wasn't with us. She had gone back into the kitchen to 'wash dishes,' but I knew my Mom well enough to know that she was just using that as an excuse to get away from Dad. My parents loved each other, but it was clear to me that Dad had crossed some sort of line and Mom was using washing the dishes as an excuse to avoid getting into a fight with him about it.

"All right, Kevin," said Dad. "I know this is very abrupt, but I intended to tell you about my identity as Genius at some point."

The shock in my brain seemed to have finally faded, because I finally found the words to say, "You mean this isn't a joke?"

"Of course not," said Dad, shaking his head. He patted the helmet on his lap. "This helmet and suit are the same helmet and suit worn by Genius during his superhero days, a one of a kind ensemble I designed for myself, although I have made a few adjustments to it over the years even after I retired from crime-fighting."

I was still convinced that this was some kind of hallucination (maybe caused by the bad cafeteria food). "But … I don't understand. You're not a superhero. You're, well, you're just my Dad, an ordinary software developer. Right?"

Dad chuckled. "Technically, you're correct. I *am* a software developer, one of the best in the world, but before I did that, I was the superhero Genius."

At this point, I was sure that maybe Dad really was pulling off some sort of elaborate and epic prank. Genius was a legendary superhero, one of the very first neoheroes that appeared thirty years ago when Haley's Comet flew by the Earth and activated the neogene in humanity. Genius had only been 11-years-old at the time—the youngest neohero in the world—but had used his super intelligence to save the world on more than one occasion and had even been one of the founding members of the Neohero Alliance. He had defeated or helped defeat villains like Nuclear Winter and Master Chaos, among others.

THE SUPERHERO'S TEST

The only reason I knew all of that was because we had been taught about neohero history in school. Also, Dad had a lot of books about the history and science of neoheroes scattered around the house and I had read more than a few when I was a kid.

Yet there was no way that my boring, ordinary Dad was *that* Genius, the Genius who was friends with Omega Man, Lady Amazon, and tons of other famous neoheroes. It didn't make any sense.

"Have you been fighting crime on the side?" I said. "I mean, while I've been at school, have you been fighting crime and stuff and then getting home before dinner every day?"

Dad shook his head. "Nope. Whenever you're at school, I'm at work, except for today. I have never done any superhero antics while being your father, though I've helped more than a few of my old neohero friends with certain problems beyond their abilities since my retirement."

"I don't get it," I said. "Are you telling me that you retired when I was born?"

"More or less," said Dad, nodding. "I decided that I wanted to raise you with your mother rather than spending my days fighting the various supervillains that seemed to crop up every week."

"Mom knew?" I said in shock.

"Of course she did," said Dad. "Well, she didn't know, at first, until we got married. I was worried that she might want a divorce after that, but she accepted it, though she never liked it."

I looked back at the kitchen, where I heard the sink running and the clinking of dishes together. "She didn't seem very accepting of it earlier."

Dad frowned. "Because after I retired from crime-fighting as

Genius and resigned from the Neohero 'Alliance, I promised to her that I wouldn't wear this suit again and do superheroics. A promise I have so far kept since I retired, except for one time before this one."

I scratched the back of my head. This revelation was seriously screwing with my sense of reality, but I didn't think I was going crazy. Dad spoke as seriously about this as he spoke about anything else, and he usually spoke very seriously about everything. I couldn't just dismiss this as a joke or hallucination anymore. I had to accept reality even if it was too weird to be true.

"So why did you retire from superhero fighting?" I said, leaning back against the couch's back. "That seems pretty cool to me. A lot cooler than being a software developer, at any rate."

"Because being a superhero takes a lot more time and effort than you think," said Dad. "Juggling a family, marriage, day job or business, and crime-fighting is difficult for most neoheroes. It's why the divorce rate in the neohero community is higher than the national average."

"So you retired to settle down with Mom and raise me?" I said.

Dad nodded. "Yes. As much as I enjoyed being a superhero, raising you was far more important to me. It was hard to do, but the other members of the NHA understood and let me resign without a whole lot of fuss. I became a software developer because it keeps me out of the spotlight and lowers the chances of other people finding out my secret identity while allowing me to provide for you and your mother."

I looked at the suit Dad wore and the helmet in his lap. "But

26

you still kept the suit."

Dad shrugged sheepishly. "Well, just because I'm retired doesn't mean I have to give up my suit. I put a lot of work and effort into it and there are a lot of supervillains in the world who would love to get their hands on it, if only so they could duplicate the technology I made for it."

"But why did Mom want you to retire from crime-fighting?" I said. "Why couldn't she work while you fight the bad guys? You could have still raised me even that way, right?"

Dad looked down at his helmet, like I had asked a question that he was not sure how to answer. "Well … she was worried for my safety. She was worried that I might get killed and she would have to raise you on her own. I didn't want to put her through that kind of stress, so I retired after defeating Master Chaos and putting him behind bars."

Now I could tell that there was another reason Mom wanted Dad to stop crime-fighting. It was obvious. Dad wasn't looking at me and he was clearly only telling me about half of the truth. But I also knew that Dad could be tight-lipped when he wanted to, so I decided to ask him some other questions instcad.

"So you haven't done any superhero stuff at all since you retired?" I said.

"Occasionally, I get requests for help from some of old friends who are cashing in a favor," said Dad. He tapped his forehead. "My super intelligence and memory give me a unique skill set among neoheroes, but I have never gotten directly involved in superheroics since retiring except for one time, no."

"So how did you know that I had punched that Robert jerk through the cafeteria wall?" I said. "I didn't call or text you or anything like that."

"I put a tracking device on your smartphone that lets me listen to your environment," said Dad. "Based on the screams I heard, I guessed that you had knocked Robert across the room, although I wasn't sure how until I actually got there and saw the situation."

I pulled my smartphone out of my pocket and looked at it from every angle. I didn't see any tracking device on it and it didn't feel any heavier than it normally did, but Dad didn't sound like he was lying.

Looking at Dad, I said, "You mean you put a tracking device on my smartphone *without* my permission?"

Dad shrugged again. "I was worried about you. This is your first day at a new school, after all. I just wanted to make sure you didn't get into trouble. I would have removed the tracking device tonight, after you went to bed, once it became clear you didn't need my guidance."

"Dad, that is weird," I said. I held out my smartphone to him. "Get rid of that tracking device right now."

"Later," said Dad. "I don't have the tools to do it at the moment."

I scowled, but put my smartphone back into my pocket anyway. "It's still weird."

"I was just trying to make sure you were all right," said Dad. "I knew something bad was likely to happen on your first day of school, something you wouldn't be able to deal with on your own, but I couldn't just follow you around the school in person. So I came up with a way to monitor your day without having to actually be there."

"What were you afraid of happening?" I said. "Asking a girl

out and then getting rejected? You're worse than Mom sometimes, you know that?"

"I was worried about what *did* happen," said Dad, "namely, that you would suddenly manifest your superpowers and hurt someone in the process."

I raised an eyebrow. "You knew I was going to punch someone out?"

"I did not *know*, because no one can ever know the future with perfect accuracy," said Dad, shaking his head. "But the probability of you manifesting superpowers was extremely high."

"Why?" I said.

"Because you are my son," said Dad. "There is still much scientists don't know about us neoheroes, but one thing that is obvious is that our kids tend to manifest superpowers when they turn sixteen or seventeen. I thought you were due, so I was just watching for the right moment so I could help you avoid getting into trouble."

I looked down at my hands. I no longer felt as strong as I did back in the cafeteria, but if Dad was right, then that power was still somewhere within me. "But I don't get it. If I inherited my powers from you, shouldn't I be super smart and great at technology like you?"

Dad shook his head again. "Not necessarily. While that is a logical inference to draw, that's not what experience and data have shown us. Most children of neoheroes like yourself usually get powers that are entirely different from their parents."

"Why?" I said. "That doesn't make any sense."

"We don't know," said Dad. "It may be that the so-called 'neogene' manifests differently in different individuals. Or there might be environmental factors that affect how an individual neohero's powers develop. There's a lot of conflicting research in that area and no one agrees on the reason for it."

"Is there any way to know ahead of time what powers children of neoheroes will develop?" I said.

"No," said Dad. He rubbed his forehead, which he always did whenever something frustrated him. "And that's what makes our children so dangerous. We don't know if you will literally sprout wings and fly away or if you will just suddenly explode for no reason in the middle of a crowd and take dozens of people with you. It's the reason why a lot of neoheroes like to homeschool their children or send them to the Neohero Alliance Academy, where the sudden manifestation of their powers can be handled by experts."

"Why didn't you homeschool me or send me to the Academy?" I said. "Didn't you know that I was going to get powers like this?"

Dad suddenly frowned, like I had walked into yet another sensitive subject. "I wanted you to live a normal life, Kevin. To get the childhood I didn't get, because my powers developed at an unusually low age and alienated me from my peers. Besides, there was always the small chance that you might just be an ordinary human, because there have been reported cases of children of neoheroes who do not develop any powers of their own or develop powers and then lose them later in life."

"Is that why we moved from New York?" I said. "Because you didn't want me near Hero Island?"

"Right," said Dad. "I thought we could just live a normal life if we moved to a town that doesn't have any neoheroes or villains of its own. Silvers, Texas isn't exactly known as neohero central, unlike, say, New York or even San Francisco."

"Well, we can't live a normal life now," I said. I slumped in the couch. "Everyone in the school knows about my powers now."

"No, they don't," said Dad, staring at me like I had just said that the sky was polka-dotted. "Only you, me, and your mother know about your powers now."

"Um, Dad?" I said, returning Dad's strange look. "I punched someone all the way across the cafeteria and through a wall in front of every student in the school plus Principal Thomas and a few other faculty members. Unless everyone suffered amnesia at the exact same time, I'm pretty sure everyone knows about my powers now. And probably posted about them on the Internet, too/"

"Actually, they did suffer amnesia, of a kind," said Dad. He tapped his gauntlet. "Or rather, a memory wipe. It's a special device I designed, the only one of its kind, that allows me to alter or outright erase certain memories from people through hypnosis."

"Really?" I said in surprise. I touched the back of my head, but could not feel my memories. "How come we weren't affected?"

Dad gestured at the shades in my lap. "Those special shades protected you from its effects and my helmet's visor uses the same material to protect me from it. That's why we remember it, but no one else will."

"Won't anyone think it's kind of suspicious how Robert has a fist-shaped dent in his chest from where I hit him?" I said.

"Why would they?" said Dad in an innocent-sounding voice. "After all, you're just an ordinary high school student who just moved from New York to Texas. You're a healthy and fit young man, of course, but everyone knows that ordinary high school students can't punch their much larger classmates across the cafeteria and through the wall on the other side."

The way Dad spoke, it sounded to me like he had done this sort of thing before. It made me wonder if he had ever altered my own memories or Mom's memories before. Before today, I wouldn't have taken that idea seriously, but now, I couldn't be sure, because if Dad could keep his superhero life a secret from me, what else might he be refusing to tell me?

"So when I go back to school tomorrow, no one will call the cops on me?" I said.

"Everyone will treat you like a normal high school student," said Dad, "though I can't guarantee that the popular kids won't treat you like dirt for being the new kid. Still, no one will even suspect you had anything to do with the fact that Robert Candle is probably going to have to spend the next few weeks in the hospital. His head trauma alone will probably make him forget that you were the one who punched him."

"That's a relief," I said with a sigh. Then I looked down at my hands. "So what kind of powers do I have? Just super strength?"

"I don't know," said Dad. "Super strength is the most obvious one, but you probably have other powers we don't know about just yet. It often takes years of training before you discover and master all of your powers, but there are ways to figure them out sooner."

I looked at Dad excitedly. "So you'll be training me to use my powers? Will I get to become a superhero? With my own costume and name and everything?"

Dad bit his lower lip. He looked down at his helmet again. "Well … yes. You will need training—there's no getting around that—but I don't want you going around town fighting crime."

"What?" I said. "Why not? Isn't that what superheroes do?"

Dad looked at me sternly. "That's what adults who fully grasp the consequences of their actions do. You're not an adult yet. Being a superhero isn't all fun and games or glamor and glory. For that matter, you can't go bragging to your friends or on the Internet about your powers, either."

"Why not?" I said.

"Because neoheroes always receive unwanted attention from those who would hurt us," said Dad. "There are a lot of supervillains—and other types of people—out there who don't mind harming minors if they feel that they might be a threat to them in the future. I've known more than few younger heroes in my time who ruined, and sometimes lost, their lives by revealing their secret identities to the world before they were ready."

"But everyone knows who Omega Man is," I protested. "And he's doing all right."

"Omega Man is the most powerful neohero in the world and has thirty years of experience fighting crime and supervillains under his belt," said Dad. "Not to mention that he is the head of the NHA. He is perfectly capable of taking care of himself. You, however, are not, at least not yet."

I folded my arms across my chest. "So I can't even help other people with my powers?"

"Not until you can control them without hurting other people accidentally," said Dad firmly. "All right?"

I frowned. I was thinking about how easy it would be for me to attract hot girls if I could show off my super strength, but I couldn't rationally disagree with Dad's point. Besides, as much as I liked attention, I wasn't sure that I wanted to attract the attention of supervillains just yet.

"All right," I said, although without any enthusiasm. "When do we start training?"

"On Saturday," said Dad.

"Why not today?" I said. "I'm ready to start as soon as possible."

"Couple of reasons," said Dad, holding up two fingers. "One, you need to go back to school and get your education. I don't want you dropping out, at least not yet. And two, I need to get something for you and it will take a few days to arrive, so we won't be able to begin right away."

"What is the thing you need to order?" I said.

Dad smiled. "You'll see."

I hated it whenever Dad acted that way, but before I could interrogate him further about the thing that he needed to order for me, Mom rushed into the living room. At first, I thought she was going to shout at Dad again, but then she said, "Ted, turn on the TV. You have to see what's on the news."

I had never heard Mom speak in that tone before. She sounded terrified, like she had just seen a ghost, or something much scarier than a ghost.

Dad, however, didn't even ask her what she was so worried about. He tapped the touch screen on his gauntlet and our flat screen TV suddenly turned on to the news. It showed a pretty news anchorwoman, with the headline 'BREAKING NEWS: INFAMOUS CRIMINAL ESCAPES FROM ULTIMATE MAX PRISON' directly beneath her.

"...authorities have confirmed that Bernard Candle, also known as the infamous Master Chaos, escaped Ultimate Max prison yesterday," the anchorwoman was saying. "Master Chaos's current whereabouts are unknown, but a note was found in his cell with a message on it. The police have released pictures of the note and its contents, which police analysts are still trying to decipher."

The anchorwoman's image on the screen was replaced by a yellow sticky note, which had a single sentence on it:

I'M COMING TO AVENGE MY SON.

CHAPTER FOUR

THE IMAGE OF THE note on the screen faded and was replaced by the anchorwoman again, but then Dad turned the TV off with another tap of his gauntlet and the screen went blank.

But Mom and Dad certainly didn't have blank expressions. Mom covered her mouth with both hands, tears starting to appear in her eyes, while Dad looked like his worst nightmare had just come true. I didn't really understand it. Sure, Master Chaos was a well-known supervillain who had caused a lot of trouble over the years, but the way they acted, you'd think he was going to come after them personally.

"What do we do, Ted?" said Mom. She wiped away her tears. I hated seeing Mom look so scared. "Should we call the NHA?"

Dad shook his head. "No. As far as I know, Master Chaos doesn't know where we are. He never learned my secret identity, so we should be safe."

"Um, hello?" I said, causing Mom and Dad to look at me. "I'm feeling a bit out of the loop here. Why would Master Chaos come after us?"

Dad stroked his chin, a look of deep unease on his features. "Because I was the one who put Master Chaos behind bars sixteen-years-ago. He swore he'd come after me as soon as he got out."

"But you said he doesn't know your secret identity," I said. "That means he can't track you down. What's the problem?"

"The problem is that message he left," said Dad, folding his arms across his chest. "Did you see it?"

I nodded. "Yeah. 'I'm coming to avenge my son.' What does it mean? Is it a code?"

"That's probably what the mainstream media and police are thinking," said Dad with a sigh. "But they're giving Master Chaos too much credit. He can be clever when he wants to be, but this time, he's being straight and to the point."

"So something happened to his son?" I said. "I didn't even know he *had* a son."

"Not too many people do," said Dad.

"So what happened to his son?" I said. "Did someone kill him?"

Dad pointed at me. "*You* happened to him."

"Huh?" I said, blinking in confusion. "I don't understand. I've never even met his son."

"Actually, you have," said Dad. "His name is Robert Candle and you punched him through the wall of your school's cafeteria."

"What?" I said. "No way. That doesn't make any sense. Robert's just a bully. He's not the son of one of the most dangerous supervillains in the world."

"Actually, he is," said Dad. "I know it's hard to believe, but Robert is indeed Master Chaos's son. I've done my research. There's no denying it."

I ran my hands through my hair. "But … he doesn't have any superpowers, does he?"

"As far as I know, he doesn't, though he's at the right age to develop them soon," said Dad. "But it doesn't really matter, because Master Chaos is going to avenge him regardless."

"Avenge him?" I said. I put my hands on my chest. "Hold on. Are you saying that *I'm* Master Chaos's target?"

Dad nodded grimly. "It appears that way. I'm not sure how Master Chaos learned about you punching out his son so quickly, though. He must have some way of keeping in contact with Robert even in prison, which is odd because Ultimate Max was specifically designed to prevent prisoners from using telepathy, radio signals, and other forms of communication to contact people outside of the prison."

"But why did we move here if you know Robert was Master Chaos's son?" I said. "Didn't you worry that something like this could have happened?"

Dad shrugged. "No, mostly because no one knows who we are. I knew you'd be in the same school as Master Chaos's son, but I doubted you'd get into a fight with him or that you would be able to harm him enough to motivate Master Chaos to break out of Ultimate Max. Apparently, I was wrong."

"Honey, we need to move," said Mom, causing me to look at her. She was rubbing her hands together anxiously. "We can't stay here. If Master Chaos is after Kevin, then he's probably on his way here even now. If we move—"

"To where?" Dad interrupted her. "Ashley, I know how worried you are, but the fact is that Master Chaos doesn't give up. When he decides to kill someone, he won't stop until they're dead. We could even go to the moon and he'd find a way to get us there."

"Then we need to contact the NHA," said Mom. She sounded like she was getting a little hysterical now. "Ask them to protect us, maybe give us a few of their strongest, and—"

"And let everyone know who we are?" Dad interrupted. "I will definitely contact the NHA, and the government, too, but I think it is more important that we remain calm and think rationally about this before we do anything."

"Rationally?" Mom repeated in shock. "Master Chaos is coming after us. How can you call me irrational when you know our history with him?"

"I'm just saying that Master Chaos thrives on chaos," said Dad, holding up his hands. "And getting too emotional can throw your rational mind into chaos, so I'm just advocating that we take a moment to calm down and think this through."

"Calm down?" said Mom. "How can I calm down knowing that our son—our one and only child—is the target of … of that bastard?"

Bastard? Mom never used that kind of language before, at least around me. In fact, Mom always used to scold me whenever I used that language around her when I was young. And what was up with her tone? I knew we were in a dangerous situation now, but it seemed to me like she was taking it a bit too far.

Dad just said, "I'm just as worried for Kevin's safety as you are, but I'm just approaching it differently. Why don't you sit down so we can talk about what we need to do?"

Tears started flowing uncontrollably from Mom's eyes as she said, "Sit down and talk? We know what we need to do. We need to keep Kevin safe."

"I know," said Dad, "but—"

"I just don't want to lose another family member to that monster," said Mom.

Then, without warning, she ran from the living room again, leaving Dad and I sitting alone on the couch in awkward silence.

-

Dad told me to go to my room for now while he went and comforted Mom. I asked him what she meant about losing 'another' family member to Master Chaos, but Dad said he'd explain later and that right now he needed to comfort Mom and contact his friends in the NHA to find out what they knew about Master Chaos's escape. He didn't say anything about my training or whether we were still doing it, which frustrated me.

Nonetheless, I returned to my room and plopped down on my bed. My room was pretty bare, furniture-wise, mostly because most of my stuff was still unpacked and I was too lazy to unpack it all. I pulled out my smartphone, intending to read news reports on Master Chaos, but then I remembered how Dad had bugged it and I decided against it.

I tried to take a nap—because I was dead tired from having to get up early to go to school today—but I couldn't. Everything that had happened today kept replaying in my mind: me punching out Robert, Dad revealing that he is a legendary superhero, Master Chaos breaking out of prison and declaring to the world that he was coming after me. Moves are always stressful, but I was sure that this was not the sort of thing that happened to most kids who move from New York to Texas.

I looked up at the white ceiling, imagining Master Chaos bursting through and falling on top of me. Even though I knew about my powers, I still worried that I wasn't strong enough to defeat him. Back in his day, Master Chaos had been one of the most powerful and dangerous supervillains, evading capture from the NHA and even killing several heroes, such as the Crimson Fist. I didn't really know the full details surrounding his final defeat at the hands of Dad, but considering how seriously Dad took his return, I guessed that his first defeat hadn't exactly been a walk in the park.

How long would it take for Master Chaos to get here from Ultimate Max? I knew Ultimate Max was near New York, because it was run by both the NHA and the government, so I figured it would take him at least a few days before he got here. Of course, it could take longer if the NHA and government hunt him down, because that might force him to lay low for a while.

But that still put me—and Mom and Dad—at huge risk. Master Chaos had been active for years prior to being defeated by Dad. He had years of experience battling supers. If I went toe-to-toe with him in a fight, I doubt I'd even scratch him. I needed my training, but I wondered whether we'd even be doing that now or if we were just going to be put under government protection or something.

I couldn't handle this. I know I complained to Dad about moving to a boring Texas town in the middle of nowhere, but I didn't mean I wanted to become the target of one of the worst supervillains in the world who was apparently also a caring father. I especially hated seeing Mom so distressed, even if I didn't know exactly why she was so upset.

But I didn't know what to do, so I just lay on my bed for a while, trying but failing to sleep, before I heard a knock on my bedroom door. Sitting up, I said, "Come in."

The door opened and Dad stepped through. He wasn't wearing his Genius costume anymore; instead, he was wearing his usual blue button down shirt and black slacks. Out of his Genius suit, he resembled me even more, just older and wearing Dad clothes.

"How are you doing, Kevin?" said Dad as he closed the door behind him. "Get any rest?"

I shook my head. "No. How's Mom doing?"

Dad rubbed his forehead. "Better. I managed to calm her down and told her what I was going to do. I assured her that we would be safe and that Master Chaos would be stopped long before he set foot in Silvers, much less reach our front door."

"How can you guarantee that?" I said.

"I contacted the NHA," said Dad. "They said they're still working with the government to investigate Chaos's breakout, but they've already sent out a team to search the area around the prison for him. They think he can't have gone very far, because he just escaped recently, so they're hoping to catch him before he leaves New York."

I sighed in relief. "Whew. That's good to hear."

"Don't get too comfortable," said Dad. "There is a reason Master Chaos didn't stay captured until I caught him. He's cleverer than his name suggests. He's not quite my intellectual equal, but he's not an idiot, either."

"What are Master Chaos's powers, exactly?" I said. "I don't remember learning much about them in school."

"Master Chaos can turn any area into chaos," said Dad. "For example, once he caused a fifteen car pileup on a freeway simply by desiring for one of the drivers to lose their cool."

"So is it like reality warping or mind control?" I said.

"Both and neither," said Dad with a sigh. "Master Chaos has unique powers, to say the least. There isn't any other neohero quite like him. It seems like all he needs to do is just step into an area and will it to fall into chaos and it will."

"Is that all he can do?"

"He also has super strength," said Dad. He rubbed his face. "I learned that the hard way when I first fought him."

"So what are we going to do while the NHA and the government look for him?" I said. "Am I still going to do my training?"

Dad nodded. "Yes. While I have faith that my friends in the NHA will be able to capture him before he gets here, we still need to be prepared for his arrival. Therefore, you will need to learn how to use and control your powers so you can defend yourself if he manages to get here."

"Will he make it here?" I said.

Dad shrugged. "I don't think he should, seeing as the NHA and the government are both searching every corner of New York for him, but like I said, Chaos is smart. We need to be prepared for the worst case scenario, whatever it is."

In my opinion, the worst case scenario was that Master Chaos attacked and destroyed our house and killed us all. I wasn't quite sure how we were supposed to prepare for that, but I hated the idea of sitting around doing nothing and I was excited about the idea of learning how to use my powers, so I nodded.

"Okay, when do we start?" I said.

"We'll start your training on Saturday, like I said," said Dad. "I would prefer to do it sooner, now that Master Chaos has escaped, but I still don't have everything I need in order to train you effectively, so we'll have to wait for a little while."

"Will I still have to go to school?" I said. I was thinking about Robert and wondering if he was going to be there and, if so, whether he would remember me punching him through the cafeteria wall.

"Yes," said Dad. "Master Chaos will likely lay low for a while, at least until he is confident he can evade the NHA and the government. School is still a safe place to be for the moment, so you should go there and try to behave as normally as possible."

"Okay," I said in disappointment. "No dramatic displays of my superpowers in public to impress girls?"

"No dramatic displays of your superpowers in public to impress girls," said Dad. "Remember, superpowers are not to be shown off like expensive cars. They are meant to be used responsibly, which is why I am going to train you."

I nodded again, but I was still thinking about whether I would be able to use my powers to impress girls anyway. Super strength would probably make the girls go crazy, though I doubted I'd ever get to show off like that.

"Now today has been a long day for all of us," said Dad. "Mom is making dinner, which should be ready soon. For now, I'm going to retire to my study and order what we'll need for your training."

"All right," I said. Then I remembered something and, pulling out my smartphone, I handed it to Dad. "Hey, can you remove the tracking device from my smartphone, like you said you would?"

Dad took my smartphone and put it in his pocket. "Of course. I'll give it back to you after dinner."

"Thanks," I said.

THE SUPERHERO'S TEST

With that, Dad turned and left the room, closing the door behind him. I looked back up at the ceiling, feeling anxious about Master Chaos but excited about the fact that Dad was going to train me to be a superhero. I didn't think I'd be getting any sleep tonight.

CHAPTER FIVE

AITING UNTIL SATURDAY WAS pure torture. I was never any good at patience, but this was worse than usual, because how many kids get to be trained as superheroes? It was like waiting to go to an awesome concert you've been looking forward to all year or for Christmas, except ten times worse.

I tried to focus on school, but it was hard. Returning to school the next day, I found out that Dad was right: No one remembered what I had done. No one looked at me and ran (though the popular girls, as usual, ignored me). No one seemed afraid that I would punch them through the cafeteria wall if they annoyed me. I was treated like the new kid, like nothing strange or out of the ordinary had happened on my first day at school.

But that didn't mean there weren't any clues about what happened on my first day. The most obvious was the Robert Candle-shaped wall in the cafeteria, which had been covered with a tarp until the school could hire someone to repair it. Some of the wiser kids outlined Robert's hole and drew stupid-looking faces on the tarp, which I guess meant that Robert hadn't been exactly popular.

The biggest clue, in my opinion, however, was Robert's complete absence from school. Malcolm—who had basically become my best friend—told me that Robert suffered some pretty critical injuries from the 'air bomb' that had gone off and was going to be in the hospital for the next few weeks. That meant that I would probably not see him for a while, which was fine by me, because I didn't want to see Robert ever again. It wasn't that I was afraid of him, necessarily, because I knew I could beat him in a fight if he came after me again. It was just that I knew that Master Chaos would probably get even angrier at me if I beat his son again and I was in no mood to give him another reason to kill me.

Speaking of Master Chaos, I eagerly watched the news and kept tabs on any updates about him. So far, no one knew where he was. The NHA had members all over the country looking for him, while the government-sponsored superhero team known as the G-Men were working with them to find him. I saw a lot of the talking heads speculating endlessly about what Master Chaos's message meant and where he was going, which I guess meant that the government had not told anyone about Robert. Or maybe even the government didn't know about Chaos's son.

In any event, I kept expecting to see Master Chaos walk into my classroom any day now and attack me. I knew what he looked like, because I had searched for pictures of him on the Internet. Unfortunately, it turned out that there had been no new pictures of Master Chaos since he was thrown into Ultimate Max, so I had to rely on 16-year-old pictures that showed a man in his late thirties with wild, crazy gray hair and a mismatched outfit that made even my lame style look like the height of fashion. I figured Chaos had to look older now, though, but the news hadn't shown any new pictures of him, although I figured he'd still be recognizable if I saw him in real life.

But Master Chaos never showed up, which made it easier for me to focus on my school. Over the week, I spent every lunch period with Malcolm and Tara, who basically became my only friends at school. Neither of them mentioned me punching Robert through the cafeteria wall, which meant that they had been as affected Dad's memory altering tech as well.

Malcolm, however, couldn't stop talking about the news of Master Chaos's escape. He kept talking about how various neoheroes compared against Chaos and which one was likely to recapture him. It was from Malcolm that I learned that there was an entire subculture of teenage guys like him who spent endless time, both online and off, debating the strengths and weaknesses of different heroes and villains.

It was actually really cool. They had this tiered system called the Neo Ranks, with 10 being the strongest and 1 the weakest. The strongest heroes—such as Omega Man—were given Neo Ranks of 10, while the weakest were given Neo Ranks of 1, though there was a lot of debate and disagreement about which hero had which Rank. The villains were rated with the same system and there was an entire website, called neoranks.com, that showed where each hero and villain ranked in comparison to others.

But as fun as it was to talk about with Malcolm, I found it kind of hard to talk about because Master Chaos was apparently ranked an 8, which put him in the top 10% of all supervillains. It might have just been an arbitrary number, but the fact is that most people on Neo Ranks often had to have good reasons for assigning a neohero or villain a ranking and there were entire essays under Master Chaos's page that explained, in detail, about why he deserved to be an 8. It was actually kind of disturbing how many people gave this so much thought, like they had some sort of weird obsession with Chaos and other villains.

As for Tara, we didn't hang out or talk all that much. Sure, she still sat with Malcolm and me during lunch, but only because she was never welcomed anywhere else. She didn't seem to mind all our talk about superheroes, but I learned very quickly that you shouldn't ask her about them, because she was always very dismissive and generally had a sarcastic comment about them. I once asked Malcolm why Tara seemed so hostile toward superheroes, but he just shrugged and said she had been that way for as long as he had known her.

In any case, this was no good. Despite Tara's cold attitude, I still liked her and still wanted to ask her out, but I had to stop and think about what she would do if she found out that I had powers. That seemed incredibly unlikely to happen, because I was keeping my powers a secret from everyone, but it always felt weird whenever Tara made some snide comment about how superheroes always cause more trouble than they're worth. I just avoided the topic with her whenever we hung out together.

Dad was mysterious during the week. Every day before breakfast and every day after I got home from school, I'd ask him if the thing he ordered for me had arrived yet. He always told me no, and then I'd ask him what it was, but he'd always just say, "You'll see." Typical Dad talk, in other words.

Dad didn't seem very distressed about Master Chaos, despite how worried he had been when the news first broke. I think this was probably because Dad didn't worry very easily, but he said that he was keeping in constant contact with the NHA, who fed him all the latest details about the search for Chaos. I asked Dad if there were any updates about Chaos's location that weren't reported by the news, but Dad never gave me a straight answer about that. He'd just tell me not to worry about it and just to focus on school until Saturday.

As for Mom, she never talked about Chaos or even mentioned him. She just spent most of her time either doing housework or going out into our new community to make friends and meet people. Mom never said that she was worried or afraid, but every time I saw her whenever she thought no one was looking, there was always a mixture of fear and anger on her face. Especially whenever she looked at Dad; I could tell that she still didn't agree with his decision to train me, but she was not going to challenge his decision, at least in front of me.

I still wondered why Mom seemed so worried. Sure, I'm her son, and yes, I know moms always worry about their sons, and of course it was understandable that Mom was worried that her one and only son was the target of one of the most infamous supervillains ever, but didn't she understand that, if I learned how to use my powers, that I would be able to defend myself? It was almost like she thought that me learning how to use my powers was the real problem, not the fact that a psychotic supervillain who has killed hundreds of people is after me.

After what seem liked forever, Saturday finally arrived. I woke up earlier than usual because I was so excited to begin my training. I still had no idea what my training would consist of, exactly, because Dad had been sketchy on the details. Still, I was ready to do whatever Dad had in mind. It was probably going to be more fun than playing video games or sitting alone in my room browsing the Internet, anyway, because I didn't have any other plans for the weekend (although that was intentional on my part, because I didn't want to have a conflicting schedule).

The night before, Dad told me to meet him in the basement in the morning. So when I got up, I showered, went to the kitchen, grabbed a bagel and some coffee, said good morning to Mom, had a quick breakfast, and then went down to the basement, eager to begin my training.

I had never been down in the basement before. Well, okay, I did go down there once when we first got here, but only to move some of our boxes full of things we didn't really need to unpack just yet, like the Christmas decorations. I didn't spend much time down there, though, because I hate being underground, plus it's dark and smelly, like a rat had died down there or something.

But when I went down there today, the basement had been radically transformed. In the center of the room was a fancy-looking chair that was hooked up to a dozen different monitors of varying sizes and shapes, which showed numbers and graphs that I didn't even come close to understanding. The various boxes containing our unpacked things had been pushed up against the walls, although the smell of a dead rat was still present if much weaker than before.

Staring at the monitors was Dad, who was wearing his Genius costume, complete with helmet. Thus, I couldn't see his face, but I could see the monitors reflecting off his helmet's surface. He was typing furiously on a wireless keyboard, but I wasn't sure what he was typing. On a small table next to him was a fancy-looking suitcase that looked like the kind you stored tools in, but it had a lightning bolt-shaped logo on it, which I recognized as the logo of the Neohero Alliance.

Before I could ask why Dad had a suitcase that was from the NHA, Dad looked over the monitors at me. "Ah, Kevin. You're early. Did Mom drag you out of bed?"

"I set the alarm to get up early," I said. "I wanted to start my training as soon as possible."

Dad nodded. "Good. Please sit in the chair."

Dad gestured at the technological chair I noticed before. When I looked at it more closely, however, I noticed that it had straps on the arms and legs, which made me think of an electric chair.

"Uh, Dad?" I said, looking at Dad, who had returned to typing. "Why does that chair have straps?"

"To keep you in, of course," said Dad, which wasn't a very helpful answer.

"No, I mean, why do I need to be kept in?" I said. "What is the chair even for anyway? Where did it come from?"

"I call it the Detector," said Dad, without looking at me. "It's an invention of mine I built in the early 90s. It is supposed to be able to detect what kind of powers a neohero has. You sit in the chair, strap yourself in, and the chair scans your brain and tells you what your powers are."

"Really?" I said. "It's that accurate?"

"Well, it isn't totally accurate, of course, due to how little we know about how neoheroes' biology works," said Dad. "It has a thirty percent accuracy rate."

"Thirty percent?" I said in alarm. "That doesn't seem very accurate to me."

"It used to be ten percent when I made the first version about twenty-five years ago," said Dad without missing a beat. "The reason it is so low is because scientists still haven't completely figured out what, exactly, causes powers to form in people. I have to keep updating it whenever any new discoveries in the field of neohero biology are made and I am very proud of the progress I've made with it."

I frowned. Thirty percent might have been higher than ten percent, but it still didn't seem all that impressive to me. I was worried that it might say that I have flight powers and then Dad would push me off the top of a skyscraper as part of my 'training,' only for it to turn out that I didn't actually have the power of flight. That made me a little hesitant to sit in the Detector.

Still, I walked over to the Detector and sat in it. It was pretty comfy, despite its metallic surface, but then Dad started strapping me in before I could know what was happening. Dad tightened the straps so hard that I couldn't even feel the blood flowing through my limbs.

"Why do you need to strap me in?" I said, looking at the straps. "It's not like I'm going to get up and go anywhere."

"True, but the Detection process can be … uncomfortable at times, to put it mildly," said Dad as he put his hands on his waist, tilting his head like he was looking me over to make sure that I was strapped in well.

"Uncomfortable?" I said. "Do you mean painful?"

"No," said Dad, shaking his head. "It's just has to do with how the process works."

Dad walked over to the side of the Detector and pulled out about a large, metal bowl with blinking lights and wires attached to it.

"This is the Detection helmet," said Dad. "When you wear it, it will 'sync' with your brainwaves and feed the information it receives into my computer, which will then match up your brain waves with the brain waves of known superheroes and tell you your powers based on that."

I frowned. "I thought that neoheroes got their powers from the neogene."

"That's just a theory," said Dad dismissively. "And an old one at that, nearly discredited, since scientists have been studying neoheroes for thirty years now and still haven't been able to locate the so-called 'neogene.' Recent scientific research shows that there is something different about the brains of neoheroes and villains than normal peoples' brains, so I've based the latest incarnation of the Detector off that theory."

"Okay," I said. I looked at the Detection helmet warily. "Will the Detection helmet hurt?"

"No," said Dad. "But the Detection helmet has been known to cause disorientation after syncing with the brain. It's nothing permanent, of course, and you shouldn't worry about it, but I just thought you should be aware so you can mentally prepare yourself for it."

I bit my lower lip. "How do you know it won't, like, erase my memories or turn my brain into mush or something like that?"

"Because it hasn't done that to anyone else before," said Dad, "although I suppose there is always a first time for everything."

Before I could tell Dad that he really wasn't being a very reassuring father right now, he slammed the Detection helmet on my head and tied the strap around my chin. The Detection helmet was surprisingly light, feeling more like foam than metal, and it fit my head very well, but the wires constricted my movement.

I watched as Dad walked back over to the monitors and start typing again, no doubt getting the Detector ready to scan my brain.

"Uh, Dad?" I said as more strange numbers and graphs appeared on the monitors. "Can I ask you a question?"

"Certainly, Kevin," said Dad without looking at me. "What is it? Do you need to use the bathroom before we begin?"

"No," I said, shaking my head. "I was just wondering why we had to use this machine to figure out my powers. Can't we just, like, go out into an abandoned field somewhere and practice my powers there? I mean, we already know that I have super strength. Can't I learn my other powers through practice?"

"We learned you had super strength when you punched the son of my archenemy through the cafeteria wall and inspired said archenemy to escape from the most secure prison in the world as a result," said Dad, still without looking at me. "I don't want us doing any practical exercises yet, if only because I do not want you accidentally blowing up the house of some old man who happens to be the grandfather of some other supervillain I might have put behind bars a while ago."

"Hey, it wasn't my fault," I protested. "I just didn't know my own strength and who Robert's dad was."

"Regardless, the Detector will give us an idea of what your power range is," said Dad. "I've already told it that you have super strength, which will increase its accuracy rate by five percent."

"So it's really thirty-five percent accurate, then," I said. "That's really accurate."

I don't know if Dad sensed my sarcasm or not, because he said, "All right. I am about to start the Detection process. Are you ready?"

I nodded. "Yeah. Let's do it."

Dad nodded, but then hesitated before saying, "Kevin, I just want to let you know that I am here to help you if anything goes wrong. I doubt anything will—at least as long as I am here watching your vitals—but I just want you to know that in case you are afraid."

I wasn't very afraid. Just worried that the Detection helmet might somehow fry my brains or maybe turn me into some kind of a zombie, although it was just a minor worry.

So I said, "It's fine, Dad. I know. Just start it. These straps are getting uncomfortable."

Dad nodded again and then turned and pressed a button on the keyboard.

Immediately, I felt the Detection helmet tighten around my head. It didn't hurt, but it was uncomfortable. It felt like there was a giant plunger on my head and it was getting tighter and tighter. I would have reached up to take it off if my arms hadn't been strapped down.

But it really wasn't all that bad at the moment. I thought all of Dad's warnings were ridiculous. I was still conscious and didn't feel even slightly disoriented.

Then, without warning, my world started spinning around me. I closed my eyes, but it didn't help, because now I felt sick to my stomach. My entire body shook and shuddered, like the earth was shaking. I felt something scanning the top of my head, the top of my brain even. It almost felt like a giant hand was rubbing its fingers on my brain, which made me gasp.

"Kevin, are you all right?" said Dad, who I couldn't see due to the fact that I had closed my eyes. "Kevin, can you hear me?"

"I can," I said, but my voice was shaky. "Is it done yet?"

"Not yet," said Dad. "Just a couple more minutes and the scan of your brain waves should be complete."

A few more minutes? I didn't think I could tolerate even a few more seconds. I tried to say that to Dad, but my jaw started aching. It felt like a giant hand had wrapped around my head and was slowly crushing it between its humongous fingers.

"Just hold on a little while longer …" said Dad. "Almost done … almost …"

A sharp spike of pain was the last straw. I pulled hard at the straps holding me down and ripped them off with my super strength. Then I ripped the straps off my helmet and threw it at the other wall with a yell.

The helmet flew through the air and crashed into the wall, but it was the only thing I saw before I put my face in my hands. My head was still dizzy and I still felt sick to my stomach. My brain didn't hurt as much anymore—in fact, the pain went away as soon as I removed the helmet—but I didn't trust myself to get up and walk just yet.

Then I heard Dad run up to me and I looked up to see Dad standing above me. I couldn't see his facial expression due to his helmet, but I guessed he didn't look happy.

"Kevin, why did you throw that helmet at the wall?" said Dad. His tone was as level as always, but I knew that if I said the wrong thing, I'd regret it.

But I was also annoyed, because he seemed to be treating that helmet better than me, so I said, without caring about my sharp tone, "I threw it at the wall because it was getting me dizzy and it hurt. I felt like I was going to throw up."

Dad's hands shook, but he just shook his head and said, "You should have told me how you felt. I could have then turned off the machine and let you rest until you felt better. The process doesn't need to be done in one sitting. It can be spread out over a period of time, although its accuracy decreases by two percent due to the change in brave waves from day to day."

"I couldn't speak," I said. I rubbed my jaw, which didn't hurt anymore, but which didn't feel good, either. "You should have been paying better attention."

"I didn't know you couldn't speak," said Dad. "That's unusual. It must have interacted with your body in a unique way."

"Do I look like I care?" I said in annoyance. "I thought I was going to die."

"You were never in any real danger," said Dad. "I've used this same machine on many people in the past without any negative consequences." He glanced at the helmet, which lay on the other side of the basement. "That will cost a lot of money to fix."

"That's what you care about?" I said. "What about my health?"

"Do you feel like you need to go to the doctor?" said Dad, looking at me again.

"No," I said, shaking my head. "But—"

"Then I see nothing to be worried about," said Dad, interrupting me before I could finish speaking. "But if you want, you can go back to your room and rest while I analyze what data I managed to get from your brain before you broke the Detector."

THE SUPERHERO'S TEST

Dad's tone didn't change at all as he spoke. He almost sounded like a robot, especially with the voice distortion created by his helmet. I always knew Dad rarely showed emotion or got upset about anything, but now it annoyed me a lot.

"All right," I said. I stood up from the chair, but almost fell before catching myself, still slightly dizzy from the effects of the helmet. "Ow."

"Can you make it to your room without help?" said Dad.

I nodded. "Yeah, I think so."

Dad nodded as well and then turned and walked over to the helmet, while I made my way to the stairs. I was looking forward to taking a nap, but that didn't stop me from feeling angry at Dad for acting like my pain was no big deal.

CHAPTER SIX

AFTER LUNCH, DAD AND I returned to the basement. I didn't really want to, even though I wasn't feeling bad, but Dad assured me that I would not need to sit in the Detector again and that I would likely not need to go through something that uncomfortable and painful again. He also said that he wanted to show me the thing that he had ordered for me, which he had still told me nothing about. I wondered if it was another Detector or something.

But when I returned to the basement, I saw that the Detector was nowhere in sight. Instead, there was a single table with that same briefcase I noticed before, the one with the NHA logo on it. Dad stood beside the table, his tablet in his hand, swiping across its surface every now and then.

"Dad, what are you looking at?" I asked as I stopped in front of the table.

"The data that the Detector got from your brain waves before you broke it," said Dad, his helmeted face focused on the tablet in his hands. "It took my computers a few hours to analyze the data and put it in meaningful terms, which is why we took a lunch break."

I leaned toward Dad in excitement. "Does that mean you know what my powers are now?"

THE SUPERHERO'S TEST

"Yes," said Dad, nodding. "According to this, you have super strength, super speed, flight, and perfect memory. A very similar power set to Omega Man's, aside from the perfect memory."

"Perfect memory?" I said. "I can't even remember what I had for breakfast yesterday. Are you sure that's right?"

"As I said, the Detector isn't perfectly accurate, so it might be wrong," said Dad. "But until we receive practical evidence contradicting it, I am going to train you on the assumption that this is your power set."

I thought that was silly, but hey, Dad was the veteran superhero here and I wasn't. Besides, I liked the idea of flight and super speed, because being able to fly anywhere would be awesome.

"So I have flight?" I said. "Hold on. Let me try it now."

I jumped into the air, but then fell right back down without so much as hovering. Dad didn't look impressed by my failed attempt.

"Flight is a difficult power to master, so don't be discouraged if you can't get it right away," said Dad. "Besides, I'd rather you not fly through the ceiling and force me to spend more money renovating this house than I already have."

I guess Dad was right. I could already sort of control my super strength, but flight just didn't come to me at all.

"All right," I said. "But when we get to the practical training parts, I want to learn flight first."

"Actually, we're going to start with teaching you how to control what you already know," said Dad, "but regardless, before we can start the practical part of your training, you will need the proper equipment in order to ensure that you do not suffer any ill consequences of your powers."

"Proper equipment?" I repeated. I shuddered. "Do you mean, like, another Detector or something?"

"No," said Dad, shaking his head. He looked up from the tablet. "I mean you will need a super suit, a costume, if you will, designed especially for your body and powers. Your normal clothes are not ideal for any sort of superheroics, regardless of what you do."

I looked down at my clothes. I was wearing a black t-shirt and shorts today. "Well, I guess you're right. All of the other supers have their own costumes, but where am I going to get one of those myself?"

"You don't need to worry about that, because I've already got one for you right here," said Dad.

He placed the tablet on the table and then opened the red suitcase with the NHA logo on it. Inside the suitcase was a folded suit, but I didn't really see much of it until Dad pulled the suit out of the suitcase and held it up for me to see.

It was full body spandex, completely black, except for the red stripes that ran down the body. It even had a mask already attached to it, which had an open top for my hair and a place for my chin to jut out. It also had a set of goggles over the eyes, which looked kind of lame to me, but they didn't look removable.

"Whoa," I said, looking the suit up and down. "What is it?"

"Your super suit," said Dad simply. "It was the thing that I ordered for you, remember? I got it for you because you need it for your training."

"Wait, you can buy super suits?" I said, looking up at Dad in surprise. "Like on Amazon or something?"

"Not quite," said Dad, shaking his head. "I ordered it from the NHA. They design super suits for their members to wear. I'm technically not a member anymore, but because I am one of the Founders, they allowed me to buy a custom suit for you."

"So can anyone buy a custom suit?" I said. "Including non-members?"

"No," said Dad. "The NHA only offers super suits for their members. It's one of the perks of being an NHA member. You simply give them your size, width, and powers and they design a suit for you based on those specifications. As a result, each suit is unique, because a neohero who can set his body on fire will need a suit different from a neohero who can fly."

"Cool," I said. "But how did you order a custom suit without knowing my full powers?"

"I ordered a generic suit that can accommodate a variety of different powers," said Dad. "If we discover any new powers during your training, we can have this suit upgraded."

"Awesome," I said. "Can I put it on now?"

"Sure," said Dad. "But first, let me show you something."

Dad put the suit down on the table and then pulled something else out of the suitcase. It looked like one of those smart watches that Mr. Martin, one of my teachers back in my New York school, wore, except slightly larger. It was also silvery and shiny, like it had been polished to a sheen.

"What is it?" I said. "A smart watch? Those things are stupid."

"It's not a smart watch, although it looks like one," said Dad. "Watch."

Dad placed the smart watch on the super suit and then pressed a small, almost unnoticeable button on its side. The smart watch's screen flipped open and the super suit was sucked into it like a vacuum cleaner. In seconds, the full-sized super suit had been pulled completely inside the watch, which then closed shut and looked like it had not just absorbed a suit several times its size.

I blinked and looked at Dad. "Uh, I don't remember Mr. Martin's smart watch being able to do that."

"Because, like I said, it is not a smart watch," said Dad. "It only looks like one so it doesn't attract unnecessary attention to its wearer, which in this case is you."

"If it's not a smart watch, then what *is* it?" I said, staring at the device with uncertainty.

"Strictly speaking, it is a portable dimensional portal," said Dad. "But it's official name is the suit-up watch. It is standard wear for many neoheroes."

"What does it do, exactly?" I said. "And will I be able to get my super suit back or did it eat it?"

"The suit-up watch is a way for you to carry your super suit around without drawing attention to yourself," said Dad. "The basic idea is that, when you are not wearing your suit, it is stored in a pocket dimension that this watch is connected to. To access your suit, all you need to do is press the button on the side of the screen and the watch will shoot out your suit, which will then cover your whole body without you having to do a thing."

"Really?" I said. "But how does it connect to a pocket dimension?"

"It's far too complicated to explain here and you wouldn't understand it even if I explained it," said Dad, waving off my question. "Let's just say that it involves quantum mechanics and leave it at that."

"Did you make this?" I said, looking at the watch again, which I wasn't sure I wanted to touch because I was now worried that it might suck me into another dimension if I wasn't careful.

"Of course," said Dad. "I designed most of the tech used by the NHA. Like most of my inventions, the suit-up watch has undergone many different incarnations. This is the latest, newest, and, in my opinion, best."

"Can I try it?" I said, looking at Dad again. "Do I need to do anything first to use it or—?"

"No," said Dad. "Just strap it on your wrist like any other watch, press the button, and the watch will do the rest."

"Okay," I said.

I grabbed the watch, which felt incredibly light, even though it held my super suit in it. Well, actually, it had stored my suit in some pocket dimension, so I guess my suit technically wasn't actually *in* it, but whatever. As long as it worked, I didn't care how it worked.

Once I strapped the watch on my right wrist, I pressed the button that Dad had pressed to suck my suit into the watch.

Then the screen flipped open and my super suit shot out. But rather than go flying all over the place, it leaped at me like some kind of wild animal and clung to my body. It rapidly covered my chest, arms, legs, and head. It felt like some kind of living creature was crawling all over me, which felt disgusting.

In a second or two, the suit stopped moving and I looked down at myself to see what the suit looked like on my body.

Damn, it looked awesome. It was skintight, showing off my body. It fit so well that it was like I wasn't even wearing anything at all. In fact, my super suit felt more like a second layer of skin than a mere suit.

"So?" said Dad. "How does it feel? Can you move well?"

I rolled my shoulders, which felt just as natural as if I was not wearing the suit. "Yeah. It feels like it doesn't weigh anything."

"Yes, these super suits are indeed amazing," said Dad, putting his hands on his hips. "I designed the material that is used to create them, but the design came from NHA artists. I'm no good at making an aesthetically-pleasing design, which is why I let the artists design it."

"Cool," I said. I ran my hands down my body, feeling the smooth surface of the suit. "How well does it hold up in a fight?"

"It should protect you from most forms of attack, although you can still be hurt," said Dad. "Your super suit is designed to handle flights at one hundred miles per hour and won't wear out if you use your super speed. It is also flame retardant, so if you find yourself fighting someone who uses fire, you should be safe, although I recommend not letting yourself get set on fire for obvious reasons."

I walked away from the table, still testing out the suit's movement. Again, I was amazed at how easy it was to move in. It wasn't too tight or anything else. I couldn't wait to fly or run around in this thing. It would be amazing.

I turned around to face Dad, who still stood by the table. "Dad, this is amazing. I feel like a real superhero now."

"Glad you like it, but you're not quite there yet," said Dad. "Next, we will go onto the practical training, where we will test out your powers so you can learn how to control them."

"Does that mean we're going to go out on the streets and fight criminals?" I said. I balled my hands into fists, but mostly to test out how they felt. "I'm ready to fight crime if you are."

But then Dad shook his head again. "Sorry, Kevin, but we're not going on the streets fighting crime. That's not what I meant when I said we were going to test your powers."

"What?" I said in disappointment. "But I'm going to be a superhero. Shouldn't I learn how to use my powers by fighting actual criminals?"

"You aren't going to be a superhero," said Dad flatly. "I am only teaching you how to use your powers so you can defend yourself from Master Chaos, should he successfully make it here. You are not going to go around the streets fighting crime, especially in our little community. That's what the police are for."

"Why not?" I said. "Didn't you do that when you were my age?"

"Only because I was young and foolish," said Dad. "There is a reason I never told you about my superhero career, Kevin, and it's because I didn't want you trying to emulate it."

"But I've read about other young neoheroes who fight crime," I said. "Like the Lightning Triplets, Watt, Volt, and Lumen. They fight crime all the time and they're like fourteen-years-old each, maybe even younger."

"That's because the Lightning Triplets are not currently the target of one of the world's most dangerous supervillains," said Dad, folding his arms across his chest. "Your Mom and I want you to live a normal life. But as long as Master Chaos is after you, you will need to learn how to use your powers for self-defense."

"What's so bad about being a superhero?" I said. "They save lives all the time and even the whole world on more than a few occasions. Why wouldn't you want me to live that life?"

"Because it isn't as glamorous as it seems," said Dad. "Anyway, I do not want to talk about this with you any further. Instead, we are going to begin training right away, unless you want to continue arguing with me, and you know you can't beat me in an argument."

I would never admit it, but Dad was right. The only person who had ever beat him in an argument was Mom and I am pretty sure that the only reason she won that argument was because Dad let her. My chances of beating Dad in an argument weren't very high.

So I said, "All right. So where are we going to do the training? Here?"

Dad once again shook his head. "No. I don't want you wrecking the basement or house with your powers. Instead, we're going to a place that I think would be perfect for you to practice your powers in secret, without drawing any unnecessary attention to us from people who don't need to know about them."

"Where?" I said.

"You'll see," said Dad. He walked over to me and put a hand on my shoulder. "We're going to teleport there, so get ready."

I nodded and mentally prepared myself as Dad reached for his belt and turned the dial on it.

In an instant, the basement of our house vanished and we were standing in a wide-open, hilly field under the hot Texas sun. I looked around the area, smelling the scent of fresh grass, but did not see anyone else in the area save for us. I looked up at the sky, but it was also empty, except for a few scattered clouds.

"Where are we?" I said as I looked at Dad, who had removed

his hand from his belt and was now looking around the area like he was trying to make sure were alone.

"This is a field several miles outside of town," said Dad. "I found it during the week when I was waiting for your super suit to come in. We're out in the wilderness and there's no one nearby for miles. That's good because I didn't want anyone accidentally stumbling upon us while we practiced."

"How long are we going to practice?" I said.

"Until dinner," said Dad. "That's what I told your Mom. She'll call me when dinner is ready, so once she calls, we'll leave and resume tomorrow."

"Sounds good to me," I said. I looked up at the sky again. "I'm going to try to fly again."

I jumped into the air, but again fell to the ground. I looked up at the sky and scowled at it.

"Why can't I fly?" I said, looking at Dad again. "It's not that hard, is it?"

"It's not as easy as it looks," said Dad. "But we're not going to focus on that at the moment. Right now, we're going to focus on your super strength."

"My super strength?" I said. "Dad, I already know how to use it."

"No, you don't," said Dad, shaking his head. "Just because you have used it twice doesn't mean you know how to use it whenever you want."

"Oh, yeah?" I said. "What does that mean?"

Dad sighed, like I was being intentionally dense or something. "Consider the two scenarios under which you have used that power. What are the similarities?"

I frowned, thinking about how I had used my powers so far. "Well … the first was when I punched Robert through the cafeteria wall when he was threatening to beat me up … and then the second time, when you were using the Detector to scan my brain."

"Good," said Dad. He tapped his forehead. "But I want you to think about *why* you used your powers. What was it about Robert or the Detector that made you use your super strength?"

I thought about that. It was kind of hard because I wasn't used to this level of introspective thinking. Dad already seemed to know the answer, but I knew he wasn't going to share it with me, at least not until I gave him my best guess.

Finally, I shrugged and said, "I dunno."

Dad sighed again. "Are you sure?"

I nodded. "Yep."

"All right," said Dad, who was sounding frustrated now, although he was clearly trying to hide it. "In both circumstances, your emotions became too much for you to handle. When you punched Robert, for example, you were feeling angry at how he was treating you and how no one else backed you up, didn't you?"

"How did you know?" I said in surprise. "I didn't tell you how I felt."

"I can tell because I'm your father," said Dad. "And also because I know, from my experience with other young neoheroes your age, that it usually takes a strong emotional reaction for their powers to manifest the first time."

"And the second time," I said, quickly catching on to Dad's line of thought, "the Detector was starting to hurt me and that was making me angry and worried."

"Precisely," said Dad. "So what conclusion can we draw from these two situations?"

"That I need to be feeling negative emotions to use my powers," I said. I clinched my fists. "Become angry."

But Dad shook his head. "Wrong. The correct conclusion to draw is that you need to gain better control of your powers so you can use them for your benefit. When you punched Robert, you ended up becoming Master Chaos's number one enemy; when you broke the Detector, you cost me a lot of money. In both cases, you didn't really benefit, did you?"

I flushed when Dad mentioned that the Detector cost him a lot of money. "I didn't mean to break it."

"That's fine, but you do agree that both situations didn't work out well for you, do you?" said Dad.

"Yeah," I said.

"So you need to learn how to control your strength so you can use it to your advantage regardless of what situation you find yourself in, instead of reacting to your negative emotions," said Dad. "That is what we are going to be doing today."

"Today?" I said. "You make it sound like we're just going to focus on super strength and nothing else."

"Of course," said Dad. "It is currently the only power you have any access to and it is the one that would be most helpful if Master Chaos attacks. It is much harder to gain access to a power you haven't used before than it is to practice a power you already do have access to."

"So when will I learn how to fly and use my super speed?" I said.

"When you have completed your super strength training," Dad

said. "Anyway, enough talking. Let's get you started."

I didn't like Dad's vague answer, but it was pretty clear that he wasn't going to give me anything more detailed than that. So I looked around the field again, which was still flat and empty.

"What am I supposed to use my super strength on?" I said. I gestured at the field. "There's nothing to pick—"

A loud *boom* echoed behind me, causing me to whirl around to see a huge metal block resting on the earth just a few feet away. It was twice as tall as me and ten times as thick, but I didn't know where it had come from. It certainly hadn't been there even a second before, otherwise I would have noticed it. It was impossible to miss.

Then I saw that Dad's hand was resting on his right gauntlet, which displayed a keyboard of some sort.

"That is what you will lift," said Dad, pointing at the metal block like it had always been there. "It weighs two tons, but I think you should be able to lift it pretty easily if you are as strong as I think you are."

"Where did it come from?" I said. I looked at the sky, but didn't see anything that might have dropped the block.

"Another pocket dimension," said Dad. "I put the metal block in there for safekeeping. Once we're done for the day, it will go back into the pocket dimension until we need it again."

"Wait, so you can access pocket dimensions with your gauntlets?" I said. I looked at them with more amazement than before. "What else can they do? Cure cancer?"

"Not yet, unfortunately," said Dad with a sigh. "Regardless, you must now try to lift the metal block with your super strength."

THE SUPERHERO'S TEST

I looked at the metal block again. It looked really heavy, probably heavier than anything else I'd tried to lift in my life, but if I had super strength, then it should be easy to do.

Then I realized I had a problem and I looked at Dad again. "How do I access my super strength? Am I going to have to get angry again or something?"

Dad shook his head. "No. You should never rely on your emotions to control your powers because emotions are highly unreliable. Instead, you need to focus on accessing that strength and using it to achieve your objective."

"Focus?" I said. "How am I supposed to do that?"

"Walk up to the block, close your eyes, and then visualize yourself being strong enough to lift that block above your head," said Dad. "If you can't see yourself doing it, then you can't do it. But if you can see yourself doing it, then you can do it."

"You sound like one of those self-help books Mom always reads," I said.

"Just do it," said Dad. "Trust me. It will work."

As skeptical as I was, I decided that Dad probably knew what he was talking about better than me, so I walked up to the metal block and stood before it. Bending over, I slipped my fingers underneath it and tested its weight. Yeah, I couldn't lift it even half an inch off the ground, but I hadn't focused yet, so I closed my eyes, just as Dad said.

In my mind, I imagined myself lifting the metal block off the ground and raising it above my head. I looked pretty cool, showing off my awesome muscles as I hefted the block above my head with no problems. In fact, in my imagination, the metal block weighed almost nothing. Of course, that made sense, seeing as I have super strength.

That's how I knew I could do it. I opened my eyes and tried lifting the metal block again, certain that I would be able to lift it exactly the way I had imagined it.

But the block wouldn't even budge under my strength, no matter how hard I tried to lift it. And I didn't feel any stronger than I normally did, either.

I stood up and, looking over my shoulder at Dad, said, "I focused, just like you said I should, but I can't even budge it."

"Kevin, did you actually focus or did you instead spend time admiring yourself in your imagination?" said Dad.

I froze. "How did you know I was doing that? Can you read my mind or something?"

Dad shook his head. "No. I'm just your father and, as your father, I know you better than you know yourself."

I scowled and gestured at the block. "Then what am I supposed to do?"

"Actually focus," said Dad, tapping the side of his head. "By 'focus,' I mean simply create a mental image in your mind of you lifting the block above your head. Don't admire yourself or fall in love with your own image. Just a simple, neutral mental picture that shows you achieving your objective."

That still sounded silly to me, but I didn't know how else I was supposed to access my powers, so I decided to listen to Dad and try again.

Turning back to face the metal block, I started focusing again on making a mental image in my head of me lifting the metal block. That was pretty easy, but what was hard was not admiring my own awesome self. The mental image of myself raising that half ton metal block above my head was just way too cool for me to look at neutrally.

But I remembered what Dad had said and so I tried as best as I could to not admire how awesome it looked. I bent down in front of the metal block and slipped my fingers under it again, getting a good grip on it. I didn't feel the super strength flowing through my body yet, but I knew it was only a matter of time before I felt it.

Taking a deep breath, I began trying to lift the metal block off the ground. This time, I actually felt it budge ever-so-slightly. Excited, I opened my eyes and tried lifting it all the way above my head, but as soon as I did that, the metal block suddenly became too heavy for me to move again.

"Damn it," I said as I stood up. "I thought I got it this time."

"You were too hasty," said Dad. "You need to really focus on that mental image. It can't just be a brief moment. It needs to be in your mind long enough for it to become a part of you."

I turned to look at Dad, feeling annoyance rising in me. I wished I could see Dad's face, but his helmet made that impossible. "Why didn't you tell me that before?"

"Because I thought you would understand that," said Dad. "But I must have forgotten how hasty you are. We'll try again."

"Try again?" I said. "Can you guarantee that I will move it this time?"

"I can't, but that's because it all depends on how much effort you put into it yourself," said Dad.

"I feel like I have been doing that already," I said. "How much harder am I supposed to try?"

"It's not about working harder, but about working smarter,"

said Dad. "You see, Kevin, learning how to use your powers isn't easy. Lots of neoheroes struggle in the beginning to master their powers, even when they have a mentor to teach them. You are no different from them."

"Oh, yeah?" I said, finding it harder to control my anger. "How do you know there isn't another way to learn how to use my powers?"

"Because I've trained other neoheroes before and this method has worked with them," said Dad. "It does require some effort on the part of the student, but—"

"But it doesn't seem to work," I said in frustration. "Can we try something else?"

"Two attempts isn't when I would call it quits and start looking for alternative options," said Dad, shaking his head. "You need to try at least a few more times before we should try something else."

"Define 'a few more times,'" I said.

"As many as it will take until you are able to control your powers," said Dad.

I groaned. "Oh, come on!"

"Whining about your problems won't fix them," said Dad.

"Whining?" I said. "I'm not whining. I'm just trying to make you understand that it isn't as easy as it looks."

"Nothing worth having ever comes easy," said Dad, shaking his head. He gestured at the metal block again. "Now get back to focusing on that mental image in your head. We have no time to lose, because Master Chaos could show up any day now."

I scowled, but turned around anyway. Instead of doing what Dad told me, however, I decided I was just going to kick the stupid metal block. I was too angry to focus at the moment and I needed a way to blow off some steam. And if that pissed off Dad in the process, well, that was just a bonus.

So I kicked at the metal block as hard as I could. I expected to break my foot by kicking it, but to my shock, the metal block flew into the air. It soared through the sky before coming to a loud *crash* hundreds of feet away from where I stood with my foot still out.

I stared at the block, stunned for a moment, before looking over my shoulder at Dad. Dad, however, was not staring at the block. He was just shaking his head, his hand on his forehead, like he was starting to lose his patience.

"I didn't mean to do that," I said, lowering my foot. "I—"

"It's fine," said Dad, interrupting me before I could finish. "You got frustrated and it made you lash out. That happens pretty regularly to young neoheroes."

I sighed in relief. "So are we done for the day?"

Dad shook his head and pointed at the metal block. "Nope. Instead, we're changing up the training. Because you obviously can't lift heavy things just yet, you should instead pull that block back to where it was. You didn't kick it very far away, so it shouldn't take you very long."

I looked at the metal block again, which looked like it was partially embedded in the earth now. "Do I *have* to?"

"Yes," said Dad in a firm voice. "Now go and drag or push it."

I sighed, but started walking over to the metal block anyway. Today was going to be a *long* day.

CHAPTER SEVEN

TRAINING REALLY DIDN'T GET any better over the rest of the weekend. Although I gained better control over my super strength, it was still a lot of hard work and I still struggled with it a lot. We spent practically all day on Sunday just lifting or pushing metal blocks, only ending early so I could get enough sleep so I wouldn't be drowsy during school on Monday.

When I first learned that I had powers and that Dad was going to teach me how to use them, I was really excited. I imagined fighting criminals in the streets or at least fighting practice robots in some cool secret underground laboratory somewhere. I didn't think that most of my practice sessions would consist almost entirely of me dragging, pulling, or lifting huge metal blocks in the middle of an abandoned field in the Texas hill country while Dad criticized my every move. Hardly what I'd call exciting.

So when I woke up on Monday morning, I actually felt relieved that I had to go to school. Dad said we'd take weekdays off, although he did tell me to be home before dinner so we could review my practice sessions for improvements (which he always recorded on his gauntlets that could apparently do everything).

Because I lived in such a small town, the school was only about fifteen minutes away by foot. So I always walked there, which was kind of weird, because I was used to taking the subway to my old school back in New York. Not that I was complaining, though, because the subway was always too loud and crowded and dirty for my tastes.

But it was also very boring, because I was apparently the only kid in the entire town who walked to school. Everyone else either took the small school bus, were driven there by their parents, or drove themselves. I had a driver's license, but I didn't have a car of my own yet, mostly because I didn't need one back in New York, although now that I thought about it, I figured I would need to buy one at some point (unless I learned how to fly, that is).

The morning air was nice and cool, but I knew it would get hot soon, which is why I walked quickly. I hoped to get to the school, which was several streets away, before the heat hit, because I had learned very quickly that Texas fall was nowhere near as cold as New York fall.

Still, I hadn't had a very good breakfast this morning due to the fact that I had tried to leave in a hurry to make sure I got to school on time, so I decided to take a quick detour to the convenience store to grab a burrito or something.

So I made my way to the convenience store, which was only a little bit out of my main path to school. I had only been in it a few times before, when my family first moved to Silvers before school started, but I already had its location memorized because I liked the place.

The convenience store parking lot was almost empty, which didn't surprise me, because it was still early in the morning. But through the glass walls, I saw someone standing at the counter, a big guy wearing a ski mask for some reason. He seemed to be talking with the cashier, but I didn't sense any danger until the big guy pulled out a gun and pointed it at the cashier.

I froze. I was watching a robbery in progress. I immediately reached for my phone to call the police, just as Mom had always taught me, but then I caught myself and looked at the suit-up watch strapped to my wrist.

Could I use my powers to defeat this criminal and save that cashier's life? I know Dad said that I shouldn't try to stop criminals, but that robber didn't look like he was going to let the cashier go even if that cashier followed his every command. Even if that guy didn't kill the cashier, by the time the police got here, he might be long gone, along with all of the money and everything else he stole from the store. Besides, I was a neohero, which meant I was probably stronger than that guy and could take him in a fight.

But I couldn't suit up in public, so I sneaked around to the back side of the building until I was between the back of the store and the dumpster. It was a stinky, smelly place, but it was also the perfect place to suit up without being seen by others.

Tapping the button on the side of the watch, my suit popped out and wrapped around my whole body. In an instant, I was completely suited up, so I stood up and ran over to the store's back door, which was thankfully unlocked.

Sneaking through the convenience store's back room, I peered through the door to the main part of the store and saw that the robber was still pointing the gun at the cashier. The cashier was busily stuffing a large burlap sack full of what looked like the contents of the register and packets of cigarettes.

"Hurry, hurry," said the robber, whose hoarse, raspy voice told me why he was having the cashier fill his bag with cigarettes.

THE SUPERHERO'S TEST

"Can you move any slower? You know what I said I'd do to you if you don't fill that bag fast."

The cashier didn't say anything. He was clearly too scared of the robber to talk. It angered me to see that robber bossing around a guy who was clearly just trying to make some honest cash. That cashier was going to be the last cashier that that robber ever stole from.

So I burst out of the storage room, shouting, "Hey, jerk! Leave him alone or you'll have to answer to—"

I didn't get to finish my sentence because the robber whirled around and fired his gun at me. Because there were a few aisles of food, drinks, candy, and other assorted things you usually find in a convenience store between me and the robber, the bullet ended up hitting a bag of potato chips and sending it into the air, but I still fell down anyway just to get out of that guy's sight. My heart was hammering, because that was the first time anyone had ever shot at me; it was even louder than I thought it was going to be.

"Where did you go?" said the thug's raspy voice from the front. "Who's there? Show yourself or I'll shoot you again!"

I wasn't afraid of him at all, but I wasn't sure if my suit was bulletproof or not, so I didn't think it would be a smart thing to try rushing him. I sneaked through the aisles doubled over, listening to the robber, who as far as I could tell was still at the counter, probably because he didn't want to give the cashier a chance to escape or call the police.

"Keep filling the sack," said the robber's voice, probably addressing the terrified cashier. "Otherwise, I'll put a bullet in your brain, got it?"

All I heard in response was a terrified whimper. I took this moment to peer over the aisle to get a good look at the robber, but he must have noticed me because I heard another *bang* and a bullet whizzed by my head. I immediately dropped down to the floor, my heart hammering again as I tried to get over the shock of almost getting shot again.

"Saw you, you stupid kid," said the robber. "Why don't you come out and play? I got no problem beating snot-nosed brats like you into pulp."

Snot-nosed brats? What, did he think I was six or something?

Regardless, I didn't think I could fight him directly just yet. He still had a gun and I still wasn't sure if I could survive a bullet to the chest or other parts of my body. But then an idea occurred to me, an idea Dad would probably disagree with, but Dad would disagree with this entire situation I'm in, so his opinion didn't matter right now.

I turned to face the aisle I was hiding behind and then, pulling my fist back, punched it as hard as I could. The aisle ripped off its foundations and flew into the robber, who I only caught a glimpse of before the aisle crashed into his midsection, instantly knocking him out. His gun flew out of his hands and fell onto the floor with a clatter, but I didn't touch it, mostly because I wasn't comfortable with touching guns.

I walked up to the robber and looked at him closely. He was still breathing, which meant I hadn't killed him, thankfully, but I doubted he would be waking up anytime soon. Most likely, he was going to be out until the police arrived and arrested him.

Then I heard the click of a hammer and looked up to see another gun pointing at my face. This time, however, it was in the hands of the very scared-looking cashier, whose grip on the gun was actually very steady, even though he was obviously scared out of his mind.

"W-Who the hell are you?" said the cashier with a stutter. He nodded at the unconscious robber. "That guy's accomplice?"

"Accomplice?" I said. "Dude, I just knocked him out. I was *saving* your life. No need to shoot me."

I was almost certain that the cashier was going to pull the trigger and shoot me anyway, but then he lowered the gun and sighed in relief.

"Oh my god, I thought I was a goner there," said the cashier, wiping sweat off his forehead. "Thanks for the help."

"No problem, uh, citizen," I said, although I wasn't sure if that was exactly how superheroes were supposed to talk. "That's what neoheroes are supposed to do, after all: Protect the innocent from criminals and ensure that justice is served."

"Wait, you're a real neohero?" said the cashier. "I thought you were just some weirdo in a jumpsuit."

"Uh, yes," I said, nodding. I glanced at the clock above the store entrance and realized that school was starting in five minutes. "Uh, I must be leaving, good citizen, because I have other innocent people to save and other criminals to fight! For justice!"

I turned and ran to the storage room, but before I got very far, the cashier shouted, "Wait!"

Coming to a stop, I looked over my shoulder at the cashier, who was still standing behind the counter with his gun down, and said, in the most superhero-ish voice I could muster, "Yes, good citizen? What is it?"

"If you're a neohero, what's your name?" said the cashier.

"I've never seen you before. Are you new?"

Oh, dang. How could I forget to give myself a proper superhero name? It seemed like such an obvious thing now that the cashier mentioned it, but it still took me by surprise.

I looked around the store quickly before spotting some candy bars with the word 'BOLT' on them in big red lettering. I hadn't realized that they sold Bolt candy bars in Texas, which made my stomach growl, because I was still hungry.

"Uh …" I struggled to come up with a name. "Bolt!"

"Bolt?" said the cashier, tilting his head to the side. "Like the candy bar?"

"No," I said, shaking my head. "Like … a lightning bolt! Because like a lightning bolt, I strike hard and fast and I never strike the same place twice!"

That sounded absolutely retarded to me, but the cashier seemed impressed by it. He whipped out his phone and said, "That's so cool! Can you take a selfie with me? I want to show proof to my friends that I met a real life neohero."

"Uh, while that sounds great, I must go, citizen," I said. "Crime does not sleep and neither does justice, so I suggest you call the police so they can take that vile man to jail where he belongs. Good day!"

With that, I turned and ran out the door before the guy could ask me anything else. As much as I liked saving people, I didn't want to be late for school, not when I was still the new kid anyway. I didn't want to anger Dad even more, because if he learned that I was late to school because I beat up a criminal … well, I didn't think he'd be very appreciative of that.

CHAPTER EIGHT

Dude, did you see this?" said Malcolm in amazement as we ate together at lunch.

I looked up from my lunch at Malcolm, who was looking at something on his smartphone across from me. Tara sat to my right, as she usually did, and she still didn't seem to be paying much attention to me or anyone else.

But I ignored her for now, wondering what Malcolm wanted to show me. "What is it?"

"It's footage of some new neohero no one's ever seen before," said Malcolm excitedly. "Look, it's on YouTube."

Malcolm gave his phone to me, which I looked at curiously as the footage played. It was silent, but that didn't stop me from recognizing the robber I had beaten earlier that day, or the cashier whose life I saved. I saw the robber try to shoot me, as well me dodging the bullets and then knocking the robber out with the aisle. Still, I was almost too shocked to pay attention, because I was trying to figure out how this footage had already gotten onto the Internet.

"Where did this come from?" I said, looking up at Malcolm, who was bouncing in his seat excitedly.

"It's security footage from the local convenience store," said Malcolm as he took his phone back, the excitement in his voice obvious. "The local news station put the footage up on their YouTube channel. Apparently there was a robbery there this morning and the cashier says that a new neohero named Bolt rescued him."

I was surprised at how quickly this video had gotten put online. "Really? I've never heard of Bolt before."

"Me neither, but this is awesome," said Malcolm. He started scrolling through the comments on the video. "I didn't know we had a neohero right here in Silvers. Most neoheroes hang out in bigger cities, not small Texas towns. And look, he's already got a Neo Ranks page."

"He does?" I said, trying to act as causal as I could. "That was fast."

"Yeah, but it's missing a lot of information, like his powers, and it doesn't have a clear picture of him yet," said Malcolm. "Someone must have put it up just within the last couple of hours, after the video was put up online."

I tried not to show my surprise, because I didn't want Malcolm or Tara knowing my secret identity yet. I hadn't expected that my first crime-fighting adventure would earn me a Neo Ranks page already. I hadn't even realized that I *would* get a Neo Ranks page at all. I didn't think that Dad knew about Neo Ranks or ever visited the site or used the app, but I figured if the footage was online, then that meant he probably already knew about my little adventure.

As casually as I could, I said, "So what's his Neo Rank?"

"Uh, let me see," said Malcolm. "It's a one."

"One?" I said. I tried not to sound disappointed. "That's weak."

THE SUPERHERO'S TEST

"Well, it's only because he seems to be a new hero, since no one knew about him until today, and the most he's done so far is defeat a robber," said Malcolm. "Hardly as amazing as defeating Nuclear Winter or fighting off the Pokacu invasion."

I felt annoyed at my extremely low ranking, but I didn't say that aloud. If I was going to get in trouble when I got back home, I was hoping that I would at least get a decent ranking for it. Yeah, I knew ranks went up and down all the time on that site based on what neoheroes did and what powers they had and how people felt about them, but I didn't like being the same rank as such famous neoheroes as The Elastic Pinkie or Big Toe Man (yes, both of them exist).

"But I wonder who this Bolt guy is," said Malcolm. He was watching the security footage again. "We have a few neoheroes here in Texas, like Burn Shot, but I didn't know we had one right here in Silvers."

"Yeah, it's pretty amazing," I said as I took a bite out of my ham sandwich. "Guess this little town isn't as boring as it seems."

"It's kind of hard to tell, but Bolt looks pretty young in the footage," said Malcolm. "Maybe about our age." He suddenly raised his head and looked around the crowded, loud cafeteria. "Hey, do you think he's a student here at the school?"

I also looked around, mostly to avoid arousing Malcolm's suspicion. "I don't know. I'm still new here, remember? I don't know any of the other students well enough to guess who it might be. He might not even be a student here at all. Maybe he's homeschooled or maybe he goes to the Academy."

"Nah, the Academy is on Hero Island near New York, which is too far away," said Malcolm, shaking his head. "Besides, we know who all of the Academy students are. Their superhero names are publicly available online and Bolt's isn't among them. Nah, Bolt's clearly a new hero, probably doesn't belong to either the NHA or the INJ."

"The INJ?" I said. "What's that?"

"The Independent Neoheroes for Justice," said Malcolm. "They're another superhero team, the second largest in the US next to the NHA. They're based in California."

"Oh," I said. "I've never heard of them."

"Yeah, they aren't in the spotlight as much as the NHA," said Malcolm with a shrug. "But it doesn't really matter. Wouldn't it be awesome if this new hero is a student here at the school?"

"Yeah, it would be," I said, nodding. I looked at Tara, who didn't seem to be paying attention to the conversation. "Hey, Tara, who do you think Bolt is?"

"I think Bolt is just another dumb, glory-seeking neohero," said Tara, without missing a beat. "I wonder if he is going to pay for the damage he caused to that convenience store or if the people who own it will."

Tara's tone was as a sharp as a knife. I probably should have expected it, but it still annoyed me a little.

So I said, "Hey, Bolt saved that man's life. So what if he ended up causing a little property damage in the process? Isn't it important that he saved an innocent person and helped put a criminal behind bars?"

"It's a big deal for the people who run that store," said Tara, her tone as cold as ever. "They might not even have the money to fix it, or if they do, it will take a long time and might force them to close the store for a while, which will cost them money and maybe their entire livelihood."

"Well, I think it's great we have a new neohero right here in town anyway," I said. "Don't you feel safer knowing that we have such a strong and brave hero here willing to fight crime and protect us from supervillains?"

"That's what the police are for," said Tara. She shot me an irritated glare. "And who cares about some new neohero? We get new neoheroes literally all the time. Did you hear about that one guy in China who blew up that factory full of workers with his mind?"

"Oh, uh, no, I didn't," I said. "Did anyone survive?"

"No," said Tara, again without looking at me. "Like I said, neoheroes just cause way more trouble than they're worth. I wish they would all go away."

Tara's bluntness left me temporarily speechless. I had always known that she didn't like neoheroes very much, but her criticisms felt far more personal now. But I didn't know what to say.

So I just shrugged and said, "All right. But next time you're in trouble, I hope you don't cry out for Bolt or some other neohero to save you."

"Don't worry," said Tara. "I won't."

Something about her tone made me so angry that I was going to shout at her, but then Malcolm said, "Hey, let's not fight. Why don't we agree to disagree on this issue like we always do whenever we talk about it?"

Malcolm's conciliatory tone managed to break through the haze of my anger. I could think more clearly now and I realized that I had been crushing my empty water bottle in my hands with my super strength. I stopped doing that before anyone noticed.

"So," I said, looking at Malcolm and pointedly ignoring Tara, "who do you think is most likely Bolt?"

"I'm thinking one of the players on the football team," said Malcolm, glancing over at the table where the school's athletes ate. "I mean, Bolt moved pretty fast and he is obviously really strong. It's either Josh or Reyes, because they're the strongest and fastest members of the football team."

I nodded, glad that Malcolm apparently didn't think of me as a potential candidate. He apparently wasn't paying attention to my suit-up watch, which made sense, because it was usually hidden underneath my suit whenever I put it on. Still, I turned it around on my wrist anyway, away from Malcolm, just so he wouldn't notice it.

"Well, whoever it is, I'm sure that this won't be the last we'll hear of him," I said. "Maybe he'll even become Silvers' defender."

"Yeah, but wouldn't it be awesome if you knew who Bolt was?" said Malcolm in excitement. "Then you could legitimately say you are friends with a real neohero, instead of all that fake crap you see people brag about online about how they have dinner with Omega Man every Friday like they're good friends or something."

I was almost tempted to tell him here and now that I was Bolt, but I refrained from doing so, because I was sure that Dad would just save Master Chaos the trouble and kill me himself if I blew my secret identity like this. Of course, he might just kill me anyway after school, but I didn't want to push it.

"Yeah, that would be cool," I said. Then I looked around. "Say, have you heard anything about Robert Candle? I'm not really concerned about him, but I haven't heard any updates about him for a while."

"Last I heard, he is still in the hospital recovering from that freak air bomb accident," said Malcolm, glancing at the wall that Robert had been punched through, which had since been repaired. "No one knows when he's going to get out."

I nodded in relief. "I wonder if he'll ever be able to walk again after that."

"Dunno," said Malcolm with a shrug as he ate some of his macaroni. "Maybe he'd be less of a bully if he couldn't walk on his own two legs. All I've heard is that he's gone crazy."

I frowned. "Crazy? How?"

"Just something I overheard from one of his friends when I got to school earlier," said Malcolm. "Robert's apparently been ranting about how 'the new kid' nearly killed him with one punch. His doctors apparently think the explosion of the bomb harmed his brain, which means they might put him in a mental ward if he gets worse. Pretty crazy, huh?"

I nodded again and tried not to show any fear, but it was hard. I knew that Robert had been the only person in the school to avoid Dad's memory-wiping gauntlet. I had hoped, however, that punching him through the wall of the cafeteria would have harmed his memory, but if Malcolm was telling the truth, then Robert remembered full well how he had really ended up in the hospital.

Of course, it sounded like no one really believed him, but how long would it take for someone to make the connection between his rantings and my appearance as Bolt, which was now on the Internet for everyone to see?

That was it. If I was going to make sure that I kept my identity a secret, I would have to go to Robert's hospital room and use Dad's gauntlet to wipe his memory of me punching him through the cafeteria wall.

After, of course, Dad killed me for doing the exact thing I wasn't supposed to do and got caught on camera doing it.

CHAPTER NINE

WHEN I GOT HOME after school—far too fast for my tastes, because this time, there weren't any convenience stores being robbed that I could use as an excuse for being late—Dad was sitting in the living room, although he was not in his Genius costume. Instead, he wore his usual blue button down shirt and black slacks, his horn-rimmed glasses reflecting the video playing on the tablet he held in his hands.

Stopping in the entrance to the living room, with my backpack slung over my shoulder, I tried to look as casual and innocent as possible. Dad didn't seem to have noticed me yet, but I knew that was bull, because Dad was always aware of his surroundings even if you weren't.

"So, uh …" I said, my voice trailing off as I tried to figure out what to say. "I'm home from school."

Dad didn't look up at me; he reminded me of Tara, actually, with the way he focused on the tablet, which was similar to how she focused on her smartphone. He just said, "Kevin, please come in and sit down. There's something I want to talk with you about."

There it was. That was Dad's 'I'm-not-angry-just-disappointed' tone. He only used it whenever I *really* disappointed him.

Part of me wanted to run into my room and hide in there, but I walked into the living room nonetheless and plopped into the large armchair to the left of the couch. I placed my backpack on the floor, but then Dad looked at me, disappointment obvious behind his eyes.

"Kevin, do you remember what I told you during our training?" said Dad. "About what you should never use your powers to do?"

I couldn't meet Dad's gaze, even though I wasn't ashamed of the good things I had done today. "Not show them off to impress girls."

Dad sighed. "No, the *other* thing you should never use your powers for."

"Fight crime," I said, again without looking Dad in the eyes.

"Exactly," said Dad. "So why did you do exactly that? And why does everyone on the Internet now know your name?"

"They don't know my *real* name," I said. "Just my superhero name."

"That's not the point," said Dad, shaking his head. "The point, Kevin, is that I explicitly told you *not* to go around fighting crime with your powers. You are only supposed to use your powers during training or in self-defense, and beating up that criminal was neither."

"But I couldn't just walk away and let him rob that store and maybe even kill that cashier," I said. I started adjusting my watch's strap, just so I wouldn't have to look at Dad in the eyes. "That wouldn't have been the right thing to do."

"You could have called the police," said Dad.

"And wait for them to get there?" I said. "Look, Dad, I know I didn't do what you wanted me to, but—"

THE SUPERHERO'S TEST

"But nothing," Dad said, interrupting me before I could finish. He looked at the tablet again and sighed. "It's even worse because you were caught on camera. And you apparently also have a page on this website called 'Neo Ranks' as well. Ever heard of it?"

I nodded, though I was thinking just how much it sucked that Dad apparently actually did know about Neo Ranks.

"Granted, it appears that no one knows your secret identity, but I still don't approve of it," said Dad. "You could have gotten yourself killed."

"He was just a normal thug," I said. "Yeah, he had a gun, but I bet his bullets wouldn't have hurt me."

"Your suit is bulletproof, but that doesn't mean a thing," said Dad. "It only takes one bullet in the right place to kill a person and if you hadn't been quick, you could have found that out the hard way."

"Well, what do you want me to do, then?" I said, finally meeting Dad's disappointed gaze. "It's too late now. I can't go back in time and stop myself from doing the right thing and saving an innocent person's life."

"I know you can't," said Dad, "but I don't want you doing something like that again."

"Okay, I won't do it again, then," I said. "Next time I see some thug robbing an innocent person, I'll just keep on walking like I didn't see anything."

"Don't act that way," said Dad. "You know that's not what I mean. I just don't want you to get involved in the superhero life, not yet. I just care about you. Why can't you understand that?"

Dad's tone made it hard to argue with him. I knew I had done the wrong thing, but I didn't know what to say. I just folded my arms across my chest and glanced at the kitchen, which seemed to be empty at the moment.

"Where's Mom?" I said, looking at Dad again. "Is she home?"

"She went to go pick up some groceries," said Dad. "She likely won't be back until dinnertime."

"What does Mom think about what I did?" I said.

"I actually learned about your little adventure from her," said Dad. "And she wasn't very happy about it. She expressed a lot of the same concerns that I did, that it was reckless, that you could have been killed, and that you shouldn't have done it."

"Of course," I said. "I knew Mom would say something like that. She's just as much against my training as you are."

"Actually, she was very much against your training, while I am not," said Dad. "If I was really against your training, I wouldn't even be training you at all."

"Yeah, right," I said. I ran a hand through my hair. "Then why can't you guys let me practice fighting *actual* criminals? I don't need to fight supervillains like Master Chaos or anything. Just normal, run-of-the-mill criminals like that thug I knocked out earlier today. Don't you think that would prepare me for combat with Master Chaos better than throwing big metal blocks around?"

Dad lowered the tablet onto the coffee table and steepled his fingers together. He was staring at the tablet, even though the screen was blank, like he was trying to move it with his mind. Frankly, I wouldn't have been surprised if Dad *could* move it with his mind. He probably had all kinds of gadgets that could do anything, even if he wasn't currently wearing his Genius costume.

Finally, Dad looked at me and said, "Do you remember your

THE SUPERHERO'S TEST

Uncle Jake?"

I shook my head. "No, but Mom told me about him. He was her brother and died a few months after I was born, right?"

Dad nodded. "Exactly. But you've seen the pictures of him, right?"

"Yeah," I said. "Mom showed me some. He looked kind of like Grandpa, except younger and with red eyes. Mom always told me that Uncle Jake had a great sense of humor and a really good work ethic."

"He was indeed a remarkable man," said Dad. He smiled, which was the first time I'd seen him smile since I punched Robert through the cafeteria wall. "He was actually the one who introduced me to your mother. We became good friends while working together and he invited me to his home for one weekend. There I met his pretty sister, who I eventually married."

"Oh," I said. "How come Mom never told me that?"

"Uncle Jake is … a hard topic for her to talk about," said Dad. "I don't know if you've ever noticed, but she usually doesn't like to talk about him, and when she does, she never says much."

Dad was right. Although Mom had told me about Uncle Jake a few times in the past, she never really talked about him very much. I just assumed that it was because she had still not gotten over his death or maybe she just didn't see any point in talking about someone who was no longer alive.

"Did Mom and Uncle Jake get along when they lived?" I said. "Or did they fight? Is that why she doesn't like talking about him?"

Dad shook his head. "No. The reason Mom doesn't like to talk about Uncle Jake is the same reason she's been so worried about

Master Chaos's escape from Ultimate Max."

"What is that reason?" I said, tilting my head to the side in confusion. "I didn't know there was a connection between Uncle Jake and Master Chaos. What is it?"

Dad looked like he was not sure if he wanted to tell me this, but then he said, "Your Uncle Jake was murdered in cold blood by Master Chaos."

The temperature in the room seemed to drop a notch or two. All of my anger and annoyance at Dad for getting onto me for doing the right thing vanished. I sat forward, looking at Dad with worry than before. "Uncle Jake was murdered by Master Chaos?"

"Indeed," said Dad, sitting back in the couch. He suddenly looked a lot older, like his memories had added an extra decade or two to his life. "Just a few short months after you were born. Uncle Jake did get to see you before he died. In fact, that's why your middle name is Jake; it was your mother's and my way of honoring the man who brought us together."

"But … why?" I said. "Why did Master Chaos murder Uncle Jake? Was he just a casualty in one of Master Chaos's plans or what?"

"Kevin, do you remember what I told you about Uncle Jake?" said Dad. "How I told you that he was a police officer?"

"Yeah," I said. I paused and frowned. "Was that a lie, too?"

"No," said Dad. "He actually was a police officer when he lived. But he was also a neohero known as the Crimson Fist."

"The Crimson Fist?" I said. "I've heard of him. He could channel energy into his fist that made it glow red and allowed him to destroy anything he punched. I didn't know he was Uncle Jake, though."

THE SUPERHERO'S TEST

"No one did," said Dad. "Your uncle was what we in the neohero community called a 'mask,' which means that he did not reveal his secret identity to the world. Only a few trusted people knew his secret identity as Jake Williamson, such as your mother, and eventually myself."

"Is that how you met Uncle Jake?" I said. "While fighting crime?"

"We were both members of the Neohero Alliance," said Dad. "Despite our differing personalities and powers, we nonetheless became good friends and worked together on a variety of missions. We grew to trust one another and so eventually revealed our secret identities to each other, which is one of the most difficult thing for masks to do. He was the best man at our wedding and I would have been the best man at his, too, if he hadn't been killed."

Dad spoke nostalgically, but there was a definite sadness to his words, almost regret. It was very much unlike Dad, who was usually an emotionless robot.

"So why did Master Chaos kill Uncle Jake?" I said.

"Your uncle had been a persistent thorn in Master Chaos's side for a long time," said Dad. "In fact, Master Chaos suffered his first major defeat at your uncle's hands. So Master Chaos began to see the Crimson Fist as his archenemy, but he didn't actively try to kill your uncle until he finally lost patience with Uncle Jake and decided to kill him once and for all."

"What did he do?" I said.

"Master Chaos came up with a plan to capture and kill your uncle," said Dad. "I remember it well. There were reports of Master Chaos rampaging through Brooklyn, where your uncle and I were visiting your mother. Because we were the closest NHA members at the time, we went to stop Master Chaos or at least keep him occupied long enough for other NHA members to arrive and beat him.

"But when we got there, Master Chaos was nowhere to be seen. We thought that maybe he had learned that we were coming and had fled on his own, but then we noticed that the manhole cover to the sewers had been removed, so we went down there intending to chase him down there."

"Did you?" I said.

"He did, but it was actually a trap he set for us," said Dad. "Master Chaos and his flunkies separated us. They pinned me to the wall and broke my gauntlets so I couldn't use my tech and then ganged up on Jake. Jake fought well, but in the end, Master Chaos murdered him and left his body in the sewers to rot."

Dad spoke like he was still there in the sewers, watching as Master Chaos killed Uncle Jake in front of his eyes. In fact, Dad seemed to have forgotten that I was even there, because he wasn't even looking at me. His eyes seemed distant and unfocused, which was unusual for him, because Dad was always so focused and clearheaded.

"So he killed him?" I said. "Right before your eyes?"

Dad nodded. "I managed to free myself, but by the time I did, Master Chaos was long gone. I guess he did not think I was worth killing or maybe he was afraid of backup from the NHA coming. In any case, I returned to the surface with Jake's body in tow. I broke the news to your mother."

"Wow," I said. "Is that why you defeated Master Chaos?"

"Yes," said Dad. "After Jake's funeral, I made it my mission to track down and capture Master Chaos. It was hard because Master Chaos's chaotic powers meant that normal tracking equipment doesn't work on him, but eventually I did track him down to his headquarters and beat him once and for all. Or so I thought, anyway."

Dad sounded angry now, like just talking about Master Chaos was enough to make his blood boil. It was very strange to me, again because Dad always acted very stoic.

"It was your uncle's death that made me to decide to retire from active crime-fighting and raise you with your mother," said Dad. He removed his glasses from his face and started rubbing his eyes, which I noticed looked a little teary. "Jake never married, but he did have a girlfriend who he was planning to propose to. In fact, he planned to propose to her that very day and would have if Master Chaos hadn't attacked."

"You didn't want to miss out on raising me," I said.

"Exactly," said Dad as he put his glasses back on his face. "I had always known that the life of a neohero is dangerous, but until then I hadn't seriously realized what would happen if I died and left you and your Mom without me."

"Is that why Mom doesn't like me training?" I said. "Is it because of Uncle Jake's death?"

"Yes," said Dad. "Jake and your Mom were very close, so when he died, she was devastated. I didn't want her to go through that again, so I retired from superheroics. It was a hard decision to make, but a necessary one."

I nodded. I looked down at the floor, thinking about what Dad told me. I wished I had known about how Uncle Jake had died sooner, but I understood why my parents had not told me. It also made me rethink the superhero life; at the very least, I was now more aware of its dangers.

But I wasn't really angry at Mom or Dad for not telling me this. No, I understood why they wouldn't want to talk about how Uncle Jake died. I understood that they just wanted me to live a normal life and that they didn't want me to get involved in that sort of danger. They were just being good parents.

No, I was angry at Master Chaos. Originally, I was just scared of him, mostly scared that he was going to harm me and my family. I dreaded facing him in battle, even with my super strength, because Master Chaos was one of the most powerful supervillains in the world.

Now, however, I wanted to punch him out. I wanted to avenge my uncle. I couldn't stand the idea that the man who killed my uncle and brought so much grief to my family was still out there, free and able to do what he wanted. I felt my super strength coursing through my body, but I kept it under control so I would not flip out and start tearing the room apart.

"Now, Kevin, I don't want you going after Master Chaos," said Dad.

I looked at Dad in surprise. "How did you know I was thinking about that? Telepathy?"

"No, I just understand you," said Dad. "You and me are more alike than you might think. I can see the same desire to avenge your uncle in your eyes that I felt when I first saw that monster kill Jake."

"Then why don't we do it?" I said. I stood up. "I'm ready to go hunt that bastard down. I'll work with the NHA or the G-Men or whoever if that is what I need to do."

THE SUPERHERO'S TEST

"Because you aren't ready," said Dad, still sitting on the couch and looking up at me. "If you try to fight Master Chaos now, you *will* get killed. He's too powerful for you. I only told you about our family's connection with him because I wanted you to understand why your Mom and I do not want you to become a superhero."

"But—"

"No buts," said Dad, holding up a finger to silence me. "I knew you would react this way, but that does not justify intentionally putting your life at risk just to defeat him. Stay here and train and learn how to use your powers; that way, if he does manage to get here, you will be prepared to defend yourself from him."

Dad's logic was sound. As angry as I was, even I knew that I was no match for Master Chaos yet. It made more sense to stay here and train than to go searching for the man who killed my uncle.

But if I stayed and waited, then Master Chaos would eventually come here and harm not just me, but my family as well. I wanted to stop him before he ever even saw our house, but it was obvious that I couldn't.

So I nodded at Dad and said, "All right. I'll stay here and focus on my training, like you want me to."

Dad smiled in relief. "Wonderful. Now I think that is all we need to talk about, so if you want to go to your room, you can. I have to speak with the NHA and find out if they have any new information on Master Chaos's whereabouts."

With that, Dad stood up and left the living room, leaving me standing alone here.

But I didn't stand around forever. Hauling my backpack over my shoulder, I made my way back to my room, thinking about everything Dad told me. I hadn't been lying when I told him that I was going to stay here and not go after Master Chaos. I didn't want to create any unnecessary worry or fear for my parents, not after I learned about Uncle Jake's death and how that had affected Mom and Dad.

Yet neither could I just be a good boy and train like Dad wanted me. I wanted to do something, something that would ensure our safety. I didn't look forward to having Master Chaos show up on our front porch and break down our front door. I wanted to make sure that Master Chaos would not come to our house and harm us.

And I knew how to do it.

CHAPTER TEN

THE PLAN SEEMED SIMPLE enough: Take one of Dad's gauntlets, go to the hospital where Robert was being kept, and then use Dad's gauntlet to alter Robert's memory of me punching him and convince him that he had been hurt by something else (probably that air bomb that Dad made everyone believe had harmed him). That way, Robert would somehow tell his own father, Master Chaos, that I hadn't punched him and that might convince Master Chaos to leave me and my family alone.

But it wasn't nearly as simple as it seemed. For one, Dad did not just leave his superhero equipment lying around for anyone (read: me) to pick up and use for whatever we wanted whenever we wanted. And, while Dad could be reasonable, he was also very protective of his equipment and never let anyone use it, not even his own family members. That was how Dad was with his computer and computer software and so I assumed that that was how he was with his Genius costume and gear.

Second, I didn't even know where Dad kept his suit. I knew he didn't have a suit-up watch like me—I never saw him wearing one—so I figured he had to keep it somewhere else. My first guess was that it was in my parents' room, probably in their closet. But I never went into my parents' room, mostly because, well, it's my parents' room, and how many kids ever voluntarily go into their parents' room?

Third, I needed a way to get to the hospital where Robert was kept. I found the hospital's address after a few seconds of online searching, but according to my maps app, the hospital was nearly an hour away from where I lived. If I took the car, my parents would immediately know and my entire plan would fall apart before I even left the driveway.

And finally, Dad most likely kept his suit protected. After all, I doubt he'd want some thief to break into our house, find the suit, and then take it and use it for his own criminal purposes. I didn't know the exact security measures Dad used to protect his suit, but that didn't matter, because I figured they were most likely extremely high-tech. And I wasn't a very tech-savvy guy, to be honest.

Still, I had to do it. This was my only chance of stopping Master Chaos before he got here. According to the news, Master Chaos's whereabouts were still unknown, but it was believed that he was still somewhere in New York. I doubted that, myself, because if he was as smart as Dad said he was, then Chaos was likely already on his way here. That was why I needed to alter Robert's memory of what put him in the hospital.

But I couldn't get one of Dad's gauntlets right away. Aside from the fact that I was at school most of the day, Mom and Dad were home fairly frequently. Dad did a lot of his work at home, while Mom was a housewife who only ever left the house to do grocery shopping or run other errands that Dad and I couldn't. The weekends were definitely out, because Dad was home on the weekends to train me and we usually trained all day.

106

THE SUPERHERO'S TEST

In fact, it seemed like my plan to take Dad's gauntlet was just going to remain in my head when I got home from school Friday afternoon only to discover that the house was empty. I went into the living room, kitchen, and garage, but could not find Mom or Dad anywhere. That was odd. They were always home before me. Where were they?

That was when I saw a sticky note on the kitchen counter, next to a ham sandwich covered with plastic wrap. Confused, I walked up to the kitchen counter, plucked the note off it, and then looked closely at the note to read what it said:

KEVIN: Mom suddenly came down with bad sickness. Took her to the doctor to have her looked at. Sandwich is your dinner. Call me when you get home. No superheroics. Dad.

The note was hard to read because Dad had really bad handwriting, but having spent years reading Dad's handwriting, I managed to decipher it without much trouble.

I immediately reached for my smartphone to call Dad and ask him about Mom, but then I paused. While I did want to know how Mom was doing, a part of me realized that I was home alone and that both of my parents were probably going to be gone for several more hours at least. That meant I could go and get one of Dad's gauntlets without having to worry that I will be discovered.

Placing the note back on the kitchen counter, I made my way to Mom and Dad's room. The door was unlocked, so I opened it and stepped inside as quickly as I could, closing the door behind me as I looked around at my surroundings.

Mom and Dad had a bigger room than I did, although not by much. They had a big queen-sized bed in the middle, with a huge dresser on the left side of the room. A desk with a small lamp stood on the right side of the bed, which had Dad's tablet on it, while another a book—one of those romance novels Mom likes to read—lay on the bed on the side where Mom probably slept at night. The room smelled much nicer than mine, like lilacs, which was probably Mom's doing.

Then I spotted their closet on the right side of the room. It was closed, but did not appear to be locked, so I walked over to it as quickly as I could. I also moved silently, carefully walking over a pair of Dad's shoes on the floor. Even though there was no one in the house except for me, I still felt like I was sneaking through enemy territory, trying to avoid being caught.

When I reached the closet door, I did not open it right away. I quickly checked it to make sure that there wasn't some kind of security system hooked up to it, but as far as I could tell, the door was completely unlocked. That didn't seem like my security-obsessed Dad, but maybe Dad thought that it was unlikely that anyone would try to break into his closet. Or maybe his costume was hidden somewhere outside the house, although I wanted to make sure it really wasn't there before I searched elsewhere.

So I opened the door all the way, allowing me to see the interior of the closet. It was a walk-in, which didn't surprise me, because I entered the closet when we first moved in but before Mom and Dad unpacked all their stuff. On the right side hung Dad's clothes, while Mom's stuff was on the left, and their shoes were on the same sides as their respective clothing. Some of Mom's old purses were stacked on the upper levels, while the closet itself smelled like mothballs.

Walking inside, I looked at Dad's clothes, trying to see if his costume was hanging with his business suits. Unfortunately, I couldn't find it. It looked like Dad didn't hang his super suit with his business suit, which made sense, because that would be a huge security risk if there ever was one. That meant his costume was elsewhere, but where?

My first thought was the basement, so I turned to leave and check there, but before I did, I caught a glimpse of a red light blinking behind Mom's dresses. Wondering what it was, I pushed aside a blue dress and a yellow dress to see a blinking red light on the wall. It was very small, so small that I wondered how I noticed it blinking, but that didn't matter because I figured the suit had to be behind that light.

I reached over and pressed my hand against the space just beneath the blinking red light. The space folded over suddenly, revealing a tiny keypad with all twenty-six letters and all ten digits underneath it. An even smaller screen was built into the area just above the keypad, with the words 'PLEASE ENTER SIX CHARACTER PASSWORD' glowing on it.

Uh oh. I hadn't expected to have to crack a password puzzle. I was awful at guessing passwords; hell, I barely even remembered the passwords for my own accounts. How was I supposed to figure this one out?

But I couldn't just give up and leave, at least not yet. My hand hovered over the keypad as I thought about what the password might be. If I was Dad, what kind of six character password would I use to protect my super suit from someone who might want to take it?

I decided to start inputting random passwords. So I started typing on the keypad and pressing 'enter' after every password, only to see the words 'PASSWORD INCORRECT. ACCESS

DENIED' whenever I did. This went on for five minutes before I gave up and shook my head.

Okay, this was getting stupid. I didn't have all the time in the world to figure out what kind of super secret password Dad used to protect his suit. It was probably some kind of obscure reference to mathematics or science or maybe, if he was feeling cute (which Dad rarely did), some kind of dumb in-joke between him and Mom that was really embarrassing.

At this point, I probably should have just turned around and returned to my room. Or maybe just call Dad like the note said and find out how Mom was doing, but I couldn't give up just yet. I knew what I needed to do to protect us from Master Chaos and I was going to do it no matter what.

So, like the good son that I was, I activated my super strength and broke the keypad straight off the wall. Yeah, I knew Dad was going to be pissed at me when he found out, probably rant about how much money it was going to cost to replace it, and then maybe kill me, but once my plan worked and Master Chaos was no longer a threat to our lives, Dad would understand.

As soon as I broke the keypad, the wall pulled back and slid to the side, revealing a set of metal stairs that spiraled down into the darkness below. I figured that was where the suit was kept, so I made my way down the steps as quickly and carefully as I could. There wasn't much light to see by, so I had to be careful about where I stepped, but I still walked fast because I wasn't sure when Dad was going to get home.

When I reached the bottom of the stairs, I found yet another door, but this one was unlocked. It slid open at a touch, revealing a small, office-like room. On one side stood a desk, along with about a dozen monitors and four servers. The monitors were currently off, which made me wonder what Dad used them for. There was also a half-drunk cup of cold coffee at the desk, along with an overflowing waste paper basket under the desk and an unfinished burrito. It looked almost like Dad's home office, except darker and more technologically advanced, like Dad had gone into the future and brought back some technology with him.

On the other side stood Dad's super suit, which was in a glass container against the wall. His suit was on a mannequin of some sort, which looked kind of creepy, but I didn't care because I noticed that both of his gauntlets were attached to it. I walked up to the glass container and found a button beneath it that seemed to open it.

Pressing the button, I watched as the glass slid away, allowing cool air to rush out of the container. Shivering slightly, I reached up for the gauntlets. I took the right one, since I'm a righty, and found that it came off the mannequin's hand without any trouble.

Looking at the gauntlet in my hands, I couldn't believe how advanced it was. It looked like something out of a science-fiction movie. It had a large touch screen on it, in addition to dozens of small buttons and keys that were unmarked, probably because Dad most likely had all of their abilities and features memorized. I didn't, however, so I didn't know which one did the flashy memory-wipe thing and which ones didn't.

In fact, turning it over in my hands, I didn't even know how to turn it on. I didn't see a big red button that said 'ON' or anything else to suggest how it is supposed to work. I slipped it onto my hand to see how it would feel.

As soon as I did that, the gauntlet suddenly tightened and the touch screen suddenly activated. The words 'WELCOME, GENIUS' appeared on the screen briefly before they were replaced by what looked like the desktop screen (if a technological gauntlet can be said to have a 'desktop' screen, anyway). Actually, it looked more like a smartphone's main screen, displaying what appeared to be dozens and dozens of different apps, none of which were labeled or had any images to suggest what they might do.

"Uh …" I was hesitant to touch the screen, if only because I didn't want to accidentally blow my arm off. "Siri?"

"My name is not Siri," said a feminine, monotone voice from the gauntlet. "It is Valerie."

Startled, I stepped back and said, "Uh, okay, Valerie. Did Dad create you?"

"Dad?" said Valerie, sounding slightly confused. "What do you mean? You created me, Genius."

"What? No, I didn't," I said. "I'm not Genius."

"Oh," said Valerie. "But your DNA signature is similar to his. Who are you, then?"

"I'm his son, Kevin," I said. "But you can call me Bolt."

"Ah, yes," said Valerie. "I recall Genius telling me about you. He said that you are very headstrong and not very technologically-adept."

Geez, thanks, Dad, for talking about me with your computer behind my back, I thought, but aloud I said, "I didn't know Dad had a personal assistant."

"He created me about ten years ago in order to help maintain his suit and other technology," said Valerie. "Where is Genius, by the way?"

THE SUPERHERO'S TEST

"Uh …" I thought of a lie quick; I didn't want Valerie to know that I technically wasn't supposed to be down here. "He took Mom to the hospital. But before he left, he told me to check on his suit down here, just to make sure that it was safe and stuff."

"I see," said Valerie. "Well, that's odd, because I send hourly reports about the current status of the Lab to his smartphone, so why would he need you to come in person to check on it?"

Uh oh. I looked around for a moment, trying to come up with a good excuse, before looking back down at Valerie and saying, "Well, Dad just wanted me to familiarize myself with the Lab and see what it's like, since I've never been down here before. And, you know, just make sure his suit is okay and everything."

"Is that why you are wearing his gauntlet?" said Valerie. "To test it?"

"Yes, yeah, to test it," I said, nodding eagerly. "I was just trying to see how it worked. But more than that, Dad gave me a mission and I need your help if I am going to complete it."

"A mission?" said Valerie. "What might this mission be and how can I help?"

"I need to get to the Fallsville General Hospital, which is about an hour away from here," I said. "There's someone there whose memory I need to change."

"You mean you wish to use the Memory Hacker to change someone's memories of a specific event?" said Valerie. A blue app on the touch screen glowed when she said that, like she was indicating which app I would need to use.

"Yeah, yeah," I said, nodding. "So it's call the Memory Hacker, is it?"

"Yes," said Valerie. "The Memory Hacker is an app that can

induce a suggestive state of mind onto a person or group of people. You can then alter their memories of a particular event that you do not want them remembering. It works best on recent memories, but it can be used on earlier ones, too, although not as easily."

"Cool," I said. "I remember when Dad used it, he gave me some shades to wear so I wouldn't be affected by it."

"Those are called blank shades," said Valerie. "Anyone who wears them is entirely unaffected by the Memory Hacker's flash."

"Right," I said. "Now where are they?"

"They are in the top center drawer of Genius's desk," said Valerie. "There are four pairs."

"Thanks," I said as I turned around and walked over to the desk. I pulled open the drawer and found four pairs of blank shades, just as Valerie described, and took one out.

Closing the drawer, I said, "Okay, Valerie, so what do I need to do to use the Memory Hacker?"

"You must activate the app once you are near the person you wish to use the Memory Hacker on," said Valerie. "You must also make sure that the person who you wish to use the Hacker on has their eyes uncovered. They must also be staring at you; if they are not, then the flash's effect will be far less effective."

"Got it," I said.

This was all going a lot better than I thought. It seemed like Dad's security systems didn't consider me a threat and weren't trying to stop me. Maybe it was because I'm his son and so Valerie doesn't see any reason to treat me like a threat.

But now I faced the challenge of actually getting to the hospital. If Mom and Dad were gone, then I couldn't drive because that meant that they had taken the car. And I couldn't just walk to Robert's hospital, either, because if I did, it take me hours and by the time I got there it would probably be too late for me to enter the hospital and use the Memory Hacker on Robert.

The Detector said I had flight and super speed, but I had no idea how to access those powers at the moment. Besides, even if I could use them, I wouldn't know how to control them. If I flew, I'd probably end up flying straight through the atmosphere, and if I ran, I might run into the next state or just crash into a hard wall.

I was frustrated by this obstacle until I looked up at Dad's super suit and noticed that his utility belt—including the teleportation dial on the buckle—was still there. I didn't know how Dad's teleportation dial worked, but Valerie could probably explain it to me. I could use it to teleport to the hospital, alter Robert's memories, and then teleport back here in maybe ten minutes. If I was really fast, I could be back before Mom and Dad got home.

Just as I was about to walk over to the suit and take the utility belt, I heard the loud ringing of the front doorbell and whirled around to see that one of the monitors was on. And it showed Mom and Dad standing in front of the front door, with Dad trying to open the door while helping Mom—who looked sick—walk.

"It appears that your parents have returned from their medical emergency," said Valerie. "Shall I inform Genius of your mission?"

"Uh, no, no, no," I said, shaking my head as I walked backwards, toward the super suit, keeping my eyes on the monitor displaying Mom and Dad. "Not yet."

"Not yet?" said Valerie. "Why not?"

"Because I want, er, to surprise my parents," I said. "Yeah. Give them a really nice surprise. Because I'm a good son like that."

"I do not really understand, but I supposed it is not my place to understand humanity," said Valerie. "What do you want to do?"

I bumped up against the container and turned around to face Dad's super suit. I reached up and took the belt off the suit and quickly secured it around my waist.

"I want to teleport," I said. I patted Dad's buckle. "That's what Dad's belt buckle can do, right?"

"Of course," said Valerie. "Genius's utility belt can do many things, such as unleash a paralyzing gas that can leave people paralyzed for weeks and self-destruct if it lands in the wrong hands."

I froze. "Even if someone is wearing it?"

"Especially if someone is wearing it," said Valerie. "Genius does not want anyone getting their hands on his inventions and replicating them for their own goals. So he is perfectly willing to blow everything up if that's what he needs to do to ensure that his inventions do not end up in the hands of evil."

I was starting to rethink wearing the belt. "So you mean literally everything he owns can self-destruct?"

"Yes," said Valerie. "But do not worry. Genius makes his inventions sturdy as well as remarkable. They will only explode if he tells them to. You do not need to worry about accidentally setting them off."

I knew Valerie is an AI and all and probably couldn't feel any emotions, but she still seemed far too calm about the fact that

THE SUPERHERO'S TEST

Dad's entire superhero ensemble was basically a bomb. It made me wonder if his smartphone could explode, too.

But I had come too far now to have any second thoughts, so I said to Valerie, "Okay, Val, how does the teleportation dial work?"

"You mean the Teleportation Buckle?" said Valerie. "In order to use the Teleportation Buckle, you need to first input the desired coordinates of the place to which you wish to teleport."

I looked down at the Buckle, but it didn't make any sense to me. "Uh, how do I do that?"

A keyboard suddenly appeared on the touch screen on the gauntlet. "Just type in the address of the location to which you wish to teleport and I will send it to the Buckle, because it is connected to the gauntlet."

I quickly typed in the address for Fallsville General Hospital into the screen. A second after I hit 'enter,' Valerie said, "Fallsville General Hospital has been found. Simply twist the dial clockwise to teleport there."

That seemed too simple to me, but Valerie hadn't led me wrong so far, so I grabbed the Buckle and twisted it clockwise.

In an instant, Dad's Lab vanished around me, but then I immediately found myself standing behind the Fallsville General Hospital.

CHAPTER ELEVEN

BLINKING, I LOOKED AROUND, my head feeling a little woozy as I looked for any other people nearby who might have seen me teleport.

"Fallsville General Hospital," said Valerie, causing me to jump when I heard her voice. "How do you feel, Kevin?"

"A little sick, but I'll be fine," I said. I looked around, but did not see anyone nearby, nor were there any security cameras watching me. "Why did you teleport me to the back of the hospital?"

"So you would not be seen," said Valerie. "Genius programmed me to teleport him into the most hidden place possible, mostly so no one would see Genius teleport. I chose the back of the hospital because satellite imagery showed that it was empty; plus I believe few people come back here."

I nodded. "Good idea. I don't want anyone to know I'm here anyway."

I looked up at the back of the large hospital. It wasn't as big as the hospitals back in New York, but it was still plenty large. I stood next to the exit, but I didn't go in just yet. I realized that if I went inside now, people would see me and I would be caught on camera. And if that happened, well, my entire plan would be absolutely ruined and I'd probably get in tons of trouble.

THE SUPERHERO'S TEST

So I pressed the release button on my suit-up watch and in seconds I was Bolt, defender of humanity (still working on my title), again. But the suit did not cover Dad's utility belt or gauntlet, though that was fine by me because that made it easier for me to gain access to them.

"Okay," I said. I looked up at the hospital, squinting my eyes. "Which room is Robert's?"

"Robert's?" said Valerie. "Do you mean Robert Candle, the son of Bernard Candle, better known as Master Chaos?"

"Exactly," I said, nodding. "I came to this hospital to find him. But I don't know what floor his room is located on."

"Do you want me to access the hospital's computer systems and get you the information from there?" said Valerie.

"You can do that?" I said.

"It is a simple procedure," said Valerie. "But if you'd rather that I do not—"

"No, no," I said, shaking my head. "Do it. I really need that information right away."

"As you wish," said Valerie. "It should take me only a few seconds to hack … ah, here we are. Robert Candle, who checked into Fallsville Hospital about a week ago due to 'injuries received from a freak air bomb accident,' is on the second floor, Room Two Oh One."

"Room Two Oh One," I said. I looked up at the back of the building again, but could not tell which window was the window to Robert's room. "All right, Valerie, which window is Robert's room?"

"According to the blueprints for the hospital, Robert Candle's room is the second window from the left," said Valerie. "That is directly above us."

I looked up at the window Valerie mentioned. There was no way I could jump that high and I couldn't climb the building, either, because the hospital's exterior was too smooth and had no handholds or footholds for me to use.

Stroking my chin, I suddenly looked down at Valerie and said, "Hey, Val, can you teleport me into Robert's room? Dad used the Teleportation Buckle to teleport into my school's cafeteria. Shouldn't it be possible for you to teleport me directly into Robert's room?"

"Yes, but I heavily advise against it," said Valerie. "Teleporting directly into a room like that is hard to do with the Teleportation Buckle due to how precise your coordinates need to be in order to ensure that you do not harm yourself by accidentally teleporting into a wall or some other inanimate object."

I grimaced. "But if Dad could do it—"

"Genius has a lot of experience using the Buckle and therefore knows how to make it do dangerous things without ever putting his own life into unnecessary danger," said Valerie. "While I can't make you do anything, I highly suggest that you do not attempt it."

"Fine, fine," I said. Then another idea occurred to me. "Hey, do you have a grappling hook we could use? That might be useful."

"Sorry, but Genius did not design this gauntlet with a grappling hook," said Valerie. "I believe he did not think it would be very useful."

I sighed in annoyance and looked at Dad's utility belt. "Then he has to have something in his utility belt that can do something similar or help me get up there in some way, right?"

"No," said Valerie. "Genius used to have suction cups that he would attach to his hands and feet to allow him to scale buildings —"

"Like a spider?" I said.

"Similar," said Valerie, "but he got rid of them due to how rarely he ever needed to use them."

"So this belt has nothing that could help me scale this building, then," I said.

"Nothing at all," said Valerie. "I deeply apologize, Bolt, but unfortunately Genius only put things in there that he thought were necessary."

"It's fine, Val, it's fine," I said. "Looks like I'll just have to fly, then."

"How will you accomplish that?" said Valerie. "You do not have Genius's jet pack."

"What? Dad has a jet pack?" I said. I shook my head. "Whatever. Look, Dad told me that I have the ability to fly. So I've never used it, but if I can use it even just to hover upwards, it should help me get there."

"Flying is dangerous," said Valerie. "But if that is what you wish to do, I will not stand in your way. I will remain on standby in case you need anything."

"Thanks, Val," I said.

I looked around the area quickly, just to ensure that no one was watching, and then closed and lowered my eyes. Although I had never flown before and hadn't been trained to use my innate flying ability, I figured that it probably worked the same way as my super strength. As long as I imagined myself flying, I would be able to access the power in real life. And this time, I didn't let my attention wander, because I knew it was only a matter of time before someone stumbled upon me or, God forbid, Dad somehow caught up with me and dragged me back home.

In my mind's eye, I saw myself carefully floating up toward the window of Room 201. I imagined it with as much clarity as I could, remembering what Dad had taught me about using my super strength and applying the same principles to this exercise.

Then, much quicker than I thought, I felt my feet rise off the ground. I opened my eyes and saw that I was levitating a few inches off the ground. Even though I wasn't flying up yet, I had to admit that this was pretty damn awesome. I was almost tempted to forget about Robert and instead go flying around Fallsville like a bird, but then I reminded myself that that would be a stupid waste of time.

So I carefully floated upwards, inch by inch, never going too fast, because I worried that if I did, then I would lose control and go flying into orbit. It was actually much easier for me to fly than to use my strength. It was like I was a natural born flyer, although every now and then I'd come to an abrupt stop. It was just kind of weird, watching as the ground became smaller and smaller below me and I had no obvious way to propel myself upwards.

But I didn't question it and soon I was right in front of Room 201's window. I tried to open it, but it was locked tight. I was tempted to smash it open with my fist, but then I realized that I didn't want the hospital employees to hear me breaking in.

So I looked down at Dad's gauntlet and said, "Uh, Val? Do you have anything we could use to force open that window?"

THE SUPERHERO'S TEST

"Certainly," said Valerie. "Point the gauntlet at the window's hatch, lower your hand, and I will do the rest."

I wondered what 'the rest' was, but I didn't say that aloud. I just did what she said: Aimed the gauntlet at the window's hatch and lowered my hand.

Then a laser shot out from the gauntlet and struck the hatch. The hatch immediately snapped, prompting Valerie to say, "The window has been unlocked."

"Whoa," I said, looking at the gauntlet in surprise. "Was that a laser?"

"Yes, sir," said Valerie. "The gauntlet has a built-in laser beam that can cut through most substances. Its intensity can be increased or decreased depending on how much damage you want to inflict on the target."

I was actually starting to feel really jealous of Dad now. He had all kinds of cool gadgets and tools that were almost cooler than my own powers. I wondered if he would let me keep his gauntlet and belt after this, but then decided to worry about that later.

I lifted the window up all the way. Carefully, I hovered forward until I passed through. Then I closed the window behind me and, slowly lowering to the floor, looked around the room I had entered, just in case someone was watching me.

The room I stood in was medium-sized, with the entrance blocked off by a curtain with a floral design. A mid-sized flat screen TV was mounted on the wall, while underneath the TV was a sink and a whole bunch of medicines and other things I didn't recognize.

My attention was drawn to the bed on the other side of the

room. Or rather, to the person lying on that bed: Robert Candle, the son of Master Chaos.

Robert looked even worse than I imagined. He was in a full body cast and his head was heavily bandaged. A bunch of plastic pipes and tubing were attached to his body, which made him look like some kind of cyborg. What little of his face was still visible was nearly unrecognizable. If I hadn't known that this was Robert's room, I would have assumed that that was someone else entirely.

Thankfully, Robert was sound asleep. His eyes were closed and he was snoring slightly. I tiptoed over to his side, being careful not to make any loud noises that might attract the attention of any hospital employees just outside his room.

Stopping beside Robert, I hesitated. If I was going to change his memories, I needed him awake, but I was worried that if I woke him, he would scream and draw the attention of the hospital employees.

Steeling myself, I reached out to grab his shoulder and shake him, but before the tips of my fingers even brushed against his cast, I heard the click of the door and realized that someone was coming in.

Alarmed, I did the first thing that came to mind: I dropped to the floor and crawled under the bed. I know, it wasn't exactly the most exciting way to avoid detection, and I would probably be found out anyway, but I didn't have enough time to run or do anything else.

I got under just in time, too, because I heard the door open and then close. Lying completely still, I expected to hear the soft foot steps of one of the hospital's nurses, but instead I heard the heavy steps of what sounded like a very large man. Of course, it could have been a male nurse, but then two large boots appeared within my view, boots that didn't look like the typical footwear of your average nurse, male or female.

The two boots came over to the bed, stopping in the exact spot where I had been standing over Robert just seconds ago. I held my breath in, keeping as silent as possible, aware that the slightest noise would reveal my presence to whoever had entered the room.

Then a feminine voice with a Mexican accent said, "Robby? Robby, are you awake? It's me."

I didn't recognize the voice, but Robert must have, because I heard him wake up with a groan. I heard a little bit of movement above, but not much, probably because Robert couldn't move very much in his cast.

"M-Mother?" said Robert. His voice sounded strange, like he had lost a few teeth. "Is that you?"

Mother? Robert had a mother? Well, I supposed it made sense, seeing as Robert had a dad. I just wondered who his mother was, though. I hoped she wasn't a supervillain herself.

"Yes, Robby, it's me, your mother," said the feminine voice. "I just got off work. How are you feeling today?"

"Slightly better," said Robert. He groaned. "My spine ..."

"There, there, Robby," said his mother in a soothing voice. "It's all right. Don't make any unnecessary movements. Just rest like the doctor told you."

"Doc said I might not be able to walk again," said Robert. He sounded sadder than I had ever heard him before. "Might need to be pushed around in a wheelchair for the rest of my life. Might need someone to give me a sponge bath every day."

"I know," said his mother. "The doctor told me all about that. I wish I could take your pain away from you, but I can't."

His mother spoke with surprising tenderness. I guess I must have assumed that, because he was the son of a supervillain and was a big bully himself, that his mother would be at least as bad as he was. She almost sounded like my mom when I broke my collarbone and was recovering from it.

"All because of that new kid," said Robert. He now sounded murderously angry. "Punched me through a wall, like I was a sand bag or some shit like that. And no one believes me."

"I know, it is very frustrating, but don't worry," said his mother. Her tone suddenly became lower, like she was trying to avoid being eavesdropped. "Father is on his way to avenge you."

My eyes widened when I heard that, but I didn't move or utter even one sound. I hadn't realized that Robert's mother knew her husband had been Master Chaos, which made me wonder if she was working with him or something.

"I know he is," Robert snapped. "He's been 'on his way' for a week. I've been watching the news. No one knows where he is."

"I do," said his mother.

Robert gasped. I almost gasped myself before reminding myself that I was supposed to stay silent. I listened more closely, hoping to get some vital intelligence from Robert's mother, maybe some information I could pass onto Dad, who could then pass it onto the NHA and the government.

"You do?" said Robert. "Where is he? Is he nearby?"

"I can't tell you," said his mother. She sounded sad about that. "While I know that the walls of your room are thick, I do not want to risk someone eavesdropping on us. If they find out where your father is, then they might tell the government, and then we'll never see your father ever again."

Damn it. Looked like Robert's mother was a lot smarter than I thought. Smarter than Robert, anyway, though that wasn't saying much.

"What did Dad say?" said Robert.

"He told me that you shouldn't worry about him, that he is perfectly safe, and that he will be seeing you very soon," said his mother.

"Is that all?" said Robert in disappointment. "What did he say about the new kid?"

"Not much, because he was worried that our connection might have been compromised," said his mother. "But he did say that he has already set in motion a plan to destroy Kevin and his family. It will take a little bit of time to do, but he said that we should see the results quickly, that the world would see its results, too."

What did that mean? What plan? I didn't know Master Chaos had a plan. I listened more closely than ever, hoping that Robert's mother would slip some more information.

"Good," said Robert. He sounded deliriously happy about that. "I hope Dad catches it on video. I'd love to watch him beat that idiot into paste even if I can't be there to see it myself."

"Don't worry about that," said his mother. "Your father also mentioned that he is going to take this opportunity to make his grand reappearance in the superhuman scene."

"What does that mean?" said Robert.

"I don't know, but you know your father," said Robert's mother. She sighed dreamily. "He loves being in the spotlight. I can only imagine what kind of plan he has set in store for that kid who almost killed you."

I didn't know what was more disturbing: The idea that Master Chaos had apparently already planned out my demise or that Robert's mother was still in love with her husband, who, by the way, murdered my uncle in cold blood, and killed loads of other people, too.

"Will we get to be with Dad when he gets here?" said Robert.

"That's the plan," said his mother. "But we can't help him. The government has been watching me very closely. They think I haven't noticed—think I'm an idiot—but I know they bugged the house. I've only been able to talk to your father when I am certain that the government isn't listening."

"Do they have my room bugged?" said Robert. He sounded worried. "Are they listening in on this conversation?"

"I doubt it," said his mother. "The government knows who your father is, but they don't think you have been in contact with him. Besides, I already checked and couldn't find any bugs."

Robert sighed in relief. "That's good."

"But you are probably still being watched," said his mother. "Likely by one of the nurses in the hospital. One of them is most likely an undercover government agent. How much have you told the nurses about your father?"

"Nothing," said Robert. "I've never even mentioned my father to them. I'm not stupid."

"Excellent," said his mother. "But Robby, you must be careful. Government agents can be very slick. They could get information out of you if you are not careful. If they know that I have been in contact with your father, they could use that information against him."

THE SUPERHERO'S TEST

"I know, I know," said Robert, who sounded like me whenever I was trying to get Dad off my case. "Like I said, I'm not stupid. I'll never tell anyone about Dad ever."

"You'd better be sure about that," said his mother. "Your father's safety and freedom—and the integrity of our family—depends on you not saying a word about this to anyone outside of the family. Do you understand?"

"Yeah, I do," said Robert. "I don't want Dad to go back to jail again."

"Good," said his mother. "Neither do I. That's why we must always make sure to help him whenever we can."

"Did he say if he'll visit me soon?" said Robert.

"Your father didn't mention when he might visit you," said his mother. "But I'm sure he will. Remember, Robby, your father loves you just as much as I do, if not more so. He broke out of prison, after all, just to help you."

I heard Robert sigh. "Okay. I wish I could be out there helping him beat up that new kid."

"Yes, yes, I know, but you need to rest and recover from your injuries," said his mother. "And once you do, our family will never have to worry about the government, the NHA, or any other organization out there that wants to harm us."

Now what did *that* mean? Even if Master Chaos killed me, it seemed to me that that wouldn't make him and his family safe from the government or the NHA or whatever. Was this also part of Master Chaos's plan, the one Robert's mother mentioned earlier?

All of a sudden, a beeping noise emitted from Dad's utility belt, causing me to look down to see a blue light flickering on and off rapidly. I had no idea what that meant, but I didn't have a chance to figure it out, because in the next instant, the underside of Robert's hospital bed vanished around me.

And then I found myself lying on the floor of the Lab, staring up at a very, very angry Dad.

CHAPTER TWELVE

I DIDN'T EVEN GET a chance to explain before Dad yanked me off the floor and held me by the collar of my super suit. He looked angrier than I had ever seen him at any point in my life, even angrier than the time I accidentally deleted all his work files on his computer when I was six. And even though I was physically stronger than Dad, his anger seemed to grant him super strength, because he held me up without any hint of effort on his part.

"Dad," I said. I tried to sound as innocent and friendly as I could, but even I heard the fear in my voice. "What a coincidence. How's Mom doing?"

"Don't try to distract me," said Dad. What made his anger worse was that his voice didn't shake or tremble. It was as calm and rational as ever, which almost made me squirm under his grasp. "What the hell did you think you were doing?"

"I—"

"No excuses," Dad interrupted me. He pointed at the monitors on the wall of the Lab, which displayed the address of the Fallsville General Hospital. "What were you planning to do to Robert Candle? Kill him?"

"Sir, Kevin was simply following your orders," said Valerie, her voice speaking up from the gauntlet on my arm. "He was

131

simply trying to alter Robert Candle's memories of the time he punched him through the cafeteria wall in order to ensure the safety and well-being of you and your wife."

"Shut up, Valerie," said Dad, without looking at her. "I will talk to you later. Right now, I'm speaking with Kevin."

"Yes, sir," said Valerie before she went abruptly silent, which told me that she had gone offline. I wish she hadn't, because I really needed the backup right now.

"Now," said Dad, his eyes never leaving mine, "what did you think you were going to do?"

"I thought—"

"Don't answer that question," said Dad. "It was rhetorical. I know what you thought you were doing. I don't need an answer."

I bit my lower lip. Dad always seemed to be able to predict what I was going to say before I said it, but that didn't stop me from saying, "I don't see what you're so unhappy about. No one even saw me."

Dad laughed, a harsh, sarcastic laugh that made me want to shrink. "Kevin, you broke into my Lab, stole some of my equipment, and deceived my personal assistant into helping you attempt to alter the memories of another person, while, I might add, your mother was at the doctor for an illness. What *shouldn't* I be unhappy about?"

Hoping I could calm Dad down, I said, "Look, Dad, I know you're not happy, but that doesn't mean you need to be angry. I mean, I managed to teach myself how to fly … well, hover, really, but—"

"I don't care," said Dad. "Tell me, what would have happened if you had been seen? Do you really think that Master Chaos would not have been able to put two and two together and realize that you altered the memories of his son in order to protect your own life?"

"Well, it seemed like a—"

"Kevin, if you had done that, Master Chaos would have *known* that you are Bolt," said Dad. "As I have told you repeatedly, Master Chaos is not an idiot. He is chaotic and unpredictable, but that doesn't mean he's stupid. You, on the other hand, might be, if you thought that stealing my equipment to alter Robert's memories would have convinced Master Chaos to leave us alone."

It had never occurred to me that Master Chaos would have figured out my secret identity. "But if I had succeeded, no one would have known that I changed Robert's memories."

"You don't think Master Chaos can put two and two together and read between the lines? That he wouldn't have found it strange that his son was no longer claiming you hurt him?" said Dad. "You're lucky I managed to get you back here before you did anything *really* stupid and unfixable."

"How'd you get me back here, anyway?" I said. "You didn't have the Teleportation Buckle."

Dad nodded at the monitors. "All of my inventions are connected. It took me only a second to send a message to my utility belt telling it to come back here. Not very difficult."

"Oh," I said. "Is there anything that your inventions *can't* do?"

"Apparently, they can't make you smart," said Dad.

He let go of my suit. I stepped backwards, not because I thought Dad was going to hit me, but because Dad was so angry that I didn't want to be that close to him.

Dad held out his hand. "Give me the gauntlet and belt. Now."

I quickly detached the gauntlet from my hand and removed the belt from my waist and handed them both to Dad. Dad took them and then walked over to the glass display where his suit was kept. He put the gauntlet and belt back on the mannequin and then pressed a button that closed the container.

Then Dad turned around to look at me. He still looked angry, almost too angry, which made me wish I could leave, but I didn't, because I felt like his gaze had paralyzed me.

"Look," I said, holding up my hands. "I didn't do anything wrong. I mean, I know I shouldn't have done that, so maybe I actually did do something wrong, but trust me, I didn't have any bad intentions. I was just trying to help."

Dad raised a skeptical eyebrow. "Help? How would confirming your identity to Master Chaos 'help'? Or getting caught by hospital security and getting the attention of the government on you?"

"So the government *doesn't* know that I'm Bolt?" I said hopefully.

"To my knowledge, they don't," said Dad. "Only the NHA's highest members—my closest friends and allies—know. And that's because I did not want them sending anyone down here to attempt to recruit you to the NHA."

"You mean some people know my secret identity?" I said.

"Only a few, and they are very tight-lipped about it," said Dad, "as they are about various other secrets I've shared with them over the years. They assured me that they're going to keep the government from trying to recruit you."

"Why would the government recruit me?" I said. "I'm not that great of a superhero yet."

"It doesn't matter," said Dad, shaking his head. "What matters is that you put yourself in needless danger all so you could play the hero."

"But I wasn't 'playing' the hero," I said. "I was just trying to keep us safe."

"I know," said Dad, "but just because your intentions may have been pure does not mean that you did nothing wrong."

I couldn't argue with that. I just shrugged and said, "Well, what are you going to do, then? Take away my super suit? Ground me for a week?"

Dad shook his head. "No. Frankly, there's not much I can do to you, since your powers are burgeoning and you are almost an adult yourself. But don't think that you will get off without any punishment."

"What will it be, then?" I said.

"No more superheroics," said Dad. "Of any sort. And I will do that by having Valerie keep an eye on you and report your every move to me for a while."

"What?" I said. "But that's an invasion of my privacy."

Dad folded his arms across his chest. "Kevin, you've already proven to me that you can't be trusted to do the right thing by yourself. Besides, it won't be forever. I'll only have Valerie keep an eye on you until Master Chaos is no longer a threat to our well-being, after which I will no longer monitor your actions."

"This is unfair," I said. "I have a right to privacy."

"I'm not going to be watching you in the bathroom, if that's what you're assuming," said Dad. "You will still have *some* privacy. Just not the freedom you're so used to."

I couldn't believe what Dad was telling me, but I didn't know what to do. It wasn't like I had any authority over him. He had every right to do this, but that didn't mean I had to like it.

"What would Mom say?" I said. "Don't you think Mom would want a say in this?"

"I already discussed this with your mother, actually, before I called you back," said Dad. "She is fine with it, so you can't appeal to her for help."

I felt my super strength growing, but I controlled it. I couldn't solve this problem with my fists, which made me all the angrier. I felt so helpless and there was nothing I could do about it.

"I am sorry, Kevin, but I have to do this," said Dad. "I would prefer not, but sometimes tough punishments are necessary in order to hammer home a point."

My shoulders slumped. "Does that mean we're not going to continue my training?"

"No," said Dad. "We'll still do that, because you still need to know how to use your powers. You simply will not have the freedom to go around punching out convenience store robbers or breaking into hospitals for now."

Dad's mention of hospitals suddenly sparked a memory in my head. "Oh, Dad, I just remembered something. Back in the hospital, Robert's mother visited him and I listened in on their conversation."

"Yes?" said Dad. "What did they say?"

"Robert's mother said that she was in contact with Master Chaos," I said. "She said that Master Chaos has already put into motion a plan to destroy us. Not only that, but she said that he is going to use this plan to make his grand reappearance in the world and also protect her and Robert."

"Did she give any specifics?" said Dad. He sounded more interested than angry now.

"No," I said. "She seemed paranoid that someone might be listening in."

"Well, she wasn't wrong," said Dad. "Did she say how she was keeping in contact with Chaos?"

"No," I said. "She didn't say. She just said that she's been talking with him."

Dad looked down and stroked his chin. "We suspected that Master Chaos was likely in contact with Maria Candle, but we didn't know for sure. I will have to tell the NHA about this."

"And the government?" I said.

"The NHA can tell the government," said Dad curtly. "What troubles me is that Master Chaos apparently has some sort of plan, if Maria Candle was telling the truth. I just wish I knew what it was."

"Do you think we'll need some help?" I said. "Like, help from the NHA, maybe?"

Dad shook his head. "No. At the very least, I don't think we'll need the NHA to protect us, although I may have to install some advanced security systems in the house just in case Chaos gets here."

"Why is Maria Candle even free, anyway?" I said. "If we know that she's the wife of Master Chaos, why wasn't she arrested with him seventeen years ago?"

"Because no one even knew about her until Master Chaos was already behind bars," said Dad. "There was a big scandal when she first came out to the press as the wife of Master Chaos with

Robert as her son, but a DNA test proved that Robert was related to both. The government did investigate to see if Maria had been involved in any of Master Chaos's previous schemes, but they could not find any evidence to suggest that she had been involved in any sort of criminal activity."

"Well, I think sleeping with Master Chaos ought to count as criminal activity, if you ask me," I said. I shuddered. "I mean, have you *seen* the pictures of him?"

"Kevin, this is no time for jokes," said Dad, folding his arms across his chest. "While I am still angry with what you did, I am glad you managed to learn that Master Chaos has been in contact with Maria. This could be vital information that might be able to help us find him before he attacks us."

"So does that mean you are not going to punish me?" I said hopefully.

Dad shook his head. "Of course not. You're still getting the punishment you deserve. And yes, we will resume your training on Saturday, so don't make any plans with your friends for the weekend."

Friends? What friends? I suppose there was Malcolm and Tara, but Dad didn't know about them. He must have assumed that I had already made some friends in this small town, even though most of the kids at the school still seemed to think I was a freak.

Nonetheless, I said, "Okay. Can I go back to my room?"

Dad nodded. "Yes. But please take off your super suit. There's no need to wear it around the house."

I sighed, but pressed the button on my suit-up watch and in a second I was standing in my normal clothes again. Then I turned and walked up the steps back to the rest of the house, but slowly and without any happiness, because I knew that this next week was going to suck.

CHAPTER THIRTEEN

L IKE I THOUGHT, THIS week really did suck, mostly
because I knew that Dad was watching me. I didn't
know how, because I never saw any drones or anything
else that he could use to watch my movements, but I didn't risk
using my super powers or trying to suit up again. I just went to
school and back home every day, taking the same route without
fail.

It was a really boring week at school, mostly because the
other kids were starting to see me less as the 'new kid' and more
just like the other students. That didn't mean I became more
popular, though, or got more friends. I still ate with Malcolm and
Tara every day and didn't hang out with or talk to anyone else.

Malcolm kept speculating about the identity of Bolt every
time we sat down to talk. He seemed obsessed with my superhero
identity, probably because the idea that there was a neohero living
somewhere in Silvers blew his mind. One time he even suggested
that we hire a private detective to figure out Bolt's identity and I
wasn't sure if he was joking or not.

For what it was worth, I just listened, mostly because I
worried that if I said too much, then Malcolm would be able to
figure out my secret identity. I never had to worry about that with
Tara, though, because she never talked about Bolt or any other

neoheroes. I didn't really know what she liked, actually, except for her phone. Nor did I gather the courage to ask her out, mostly because I knew how much she hated neoheroes.

I also paid attention to my ranking on Neo Ranks. Because I had only had one public appearance so far, I was still very low, but apparently I moved up to a 1.5 at some point. The reasoning, according to the page's administrator, for the upgrade was that super strength was obviously superior to other 1 powers like having an enormous big toe, but not quite enough to raise my overall Rank to a 2 just yet. That was kind of depressing, but better than being a 1, I supposed.

But I was curious to see what Dad's ranking was. Ranks had a way of going down over the years, mostly if a neohero retired or was killed. After all, you can't gain ranks if you were dead or simply no longer fighting crime. I figured that Dad's had probably gone down quite a bit since he retired sixteen years ago.

So at lunch on Wednesday, I looked up 'Genius' on Neo Ranks only to find out that he was a 9. I gaped when I saw that, prompting Malcolm—who was sitting across from me at our lunch table rambling on about setting a trap to capture Bolt so we could unmask him—to say, "What?"

I shook my head and looked up at him. "Did you see Genius's rank? It's still a nine, even though he retired sixteen years ago."

"Oh, yeah," said Malcolm, nodding. "Well, Genius was really popular in his days, didn't you know? And he's still popular. I see discussions all the time on Neo Ranks about people wondering how Genius would handle guys like Conjurer or Hybrid. There was even a petition a while back to get him back into crime-fighting."

"Really?" I said in surprise. "Where did the petition go?"

"It was submitted to the Neohero Alliance, because they're the only people who know Genius's real identity and how to contact him," said Malcolm. "Over one hundred thousand people signed it. You can still find it online if you search."

"One hundred thousand?" I said. "I didn't know Genius was so popular."

"Yeah," said Malcolm. "I just don't get why anyone would retire with that much fame. If I was as popular as Genius, I would be a superhero for as long as I lived."

I nodded, but I was thinking about Dad. I hadn't realized just how much he had given up to raise me with Mom. If over one hundred thousand people wanted him back, I bet that was only a fraction of his real fan base. I had a hard time imagining my stern, almost emotionless Dad having any real 'fans,' but I guess he did.

"But I don't understand," I said, looking at Dad's Neo Ranks page on my phone, "how he still ranks so high even if he was really popular in his heyday."

"He beat Master Chaos," said Malcolm. "That's why. Few neoheroes have ever done anything as good as that. I mean, look at his Neo Rank page. Master Chaos killed loads of heroes before Genius stopped him, heroes like the Crimson Fist."

Suddenly, I felt a surge of emotion rise in my throat at the mention of my uncle. I blinked, feeling tears starting to form in my eyes, but managed to keep myself from actually crying.

"Kevin?" said Malcolm, who seemed to notice that something was wrong. "What's up?"

I shook my head and said, "It's nothing, I—"

I was interrupted by a small *ding*, which came from

Malcolm's phone and was likely a notification, causing him to look down at his screen. His eyes suddenly became so wide that they looked like they were about to drop out of their sockets.

"Malcolm?" I said. "What's the matter?"

"Dude," said Malcolm. He held his phone at me. "Look at this news report."

I leaned forward to read the headline, which read:

'ULTIMATE MAX ESCAPEE MASTER CHAOS MAIN SUSPECT IN THEFT OF SECRET MILITARY WEAPONRY'

I looked at Malcolm. "What does that mean?"

"I dunno, man," said Malcolm. "I didn't read the article. I just saw the headline and thought you should read it."

I took Malcolm's phone from his hands and started reading the article. It wasn't very long, but it seemed to take me forever to read it:

WASHINGTON, DC—Infamous supervillain Master Chaos, who recently escaped from the Ultimate Max prison for superhumans two weeks ago, has been confirmed to have stolen secret military weaponry, the federal government confirmed hours ago.

"We can't tell you what any of these weapons are," said Cadmus Smith, the Director of the Department of Superpowered Human Beings and Extraterrestrial Beings, who is in charge of the government team tracking down Master Chaos. "But we can confirm that Master Chaos broke into one of our bases and stole some very sensitive technology that we do not want to be in the hands of anyone, superhuman or otherwise, who is a threat to the United States of America."

The story broke yesterday as rumors on the Internet before the federal government finally confirmed the story this morning. According to the government, Master Chaos, also known as Bernard Candle, broke into a secret government facility on Monday for reasons unknown. It is only known that he stole some top-secret weapons from the facility, though the exact nature of the weapons is unknown. There were no casualties in the attack, nor was anything else of importance stolen or found missing.

It is speculated that Master Chaos had a contact on the inside who helped him get in. Congress has ordered a full investigation of the people working at the facility in order to find out who, if anyone, helped Master Chaos enter the facility.

Nonetheless, the Department of Superpowered Human Beings and Extraterrestrial Beings has come under fire from critics, who claim that this is yet another example of the Department's inability to deal with the threats it was made to deal with. Presidential nominee and founder of Plutarch Industries Adam Lucius Plutarch tweeted today that if elected President, he—

I stopped reading there, because after that it was just talking about what various politicians had to say about this and who was to blame and stuff like that. I looked up at Malcolm, a serious expression on my face.

"What does it say?" said Malcolm, leaning forward. "What did Master Chaos do?"

"All it says is that Master Chaos broke into a secret government facility and stole some top secret weapons from that facility," I said as I handed Malcolm his phone back to him. "It doesn't say where the facility was or what he stole."

"Hey, that sounds familiar," said Malcolm, scratching his chin as he started reading the article. "Yeah, I remember someone on

Neo Ranks talking about this yesterday. Said that the government was going to try to cover it up and pretend nothing happened, but that it would be a big story on social media soon."

"How did that guy know about it so fast?" I said.

"No idea," said Malcolm with a shrug. "I just thought it was crazy talk, because you get a lot of guys on Neo Ranks who 'know' things like who the Midnight Menace is. There was even someone claiming to be a Pokacu alien, but I think he was just a troll."

I nodded, but wasn't really listening to Malcolm anymore. I was too busy thinking about the weapons Master Chaos had stolen. What were they? Why did he think he'd need them? Did Dad know about this? Did Dad know what the top-secret weapons were?

It was obviously connected with Master Chaos's plan, but I still didn't see how it was all supposed to come together. It just seemed very random and made me very nervous. I doubted Master Chaos had his hands on any nukes, but I still thought that Chaos could cause a lot of, well, chaos with whatever weapons he got.

That was why it was more important than ever that I learned how to use my powers. I was eager to get back to training, because I wanted to be prepared when Master Chaos attacked.

CHAPTER FOURTEEN

O KAY, KEVIN," SAID DAD, standing across from me in the field where we were doing our training. He was in full Genius costume now, his arms folded across his chest. "Try to hover off the ground."

I looked down at the ground under my feet. I willed myself to rise off the ground, just like I had back in Fallsville earlier this week, and soon found myself floating a few inches above the ground. I looked up at Dad.

"So?" I said. "Am I doing a good job?"

"It looks like it," said Dad. "What is the highest you have flown so far?"

I scratched my chin. "Um, I dunno. I floated up to the second floor of the Fallsville General Hospital, which was like twenty or thirty feet off the ground, I think."

"Thirty feet, then," said Dad. "That's not very high, but I bet you can fly much higher than that."

I looked up at the sky apprehensively. As excited as I was to fly, I suddenly found the idea of being so high up in the sky frightening. "What will happen if I fall? Will I get hurt?"

"Probably, but I doubt it will leave you paralyzed or anything like that," said Dad. "You have super strength, after all, and most neoheroes with super strength also tend to be strong enough to survive falls even from great heights."

"Okay," I said. I pulled my goggles down over my eyes. "So how high should I go?"

"As high as possible," said Dad. "But I suggest not going into orbit. We don't know if you can survive in space without a space suit, so try to stay within the atmosphere at least."

I nodded. I looked up at the sky again, again feeling apprehensive, but I figured that if Dad was not panicking about it, then I didn't need to, either.

So I started rising again, increasing my speed bit by bit, until soon I had definitely passed the thirty foot mark and was now going higher than I ever had before. I looked down at Dad, who was looking up at me and becoming smaller and smaller with every foot I climbed.

But I looked away from the ground, because I didn't want to freak myself out. Instead, I focused on going higher and faster, and before I knew, I was soaring through the sky like a lightning bolt. Wind blew through my hair and the goggles protected my eyes from getting dried out.

It was a lot of fun, flying around in the sky. It was almost like swimming, except that I didn't need to move my limbs. I just soared through the air, passed through some clouds (which got me a little wet), and then abruptly stopped and looked down at the ground.

Bad idea. I felt woozy. I could see Dad below, but not very well. I looked up again and immediately felt better. It was weird how I apparently had the power of flight, but did not have the stomach to go with it. Or maybe it was one of those things that I'd get used to after a while.

Then I heard the earcom crackle in my ear and then Dad's voice said, "Kevin? Can you hear me? How are you doing up there?"

I cringed slightly at the volume of the earpiece, but said, "Okay. I can't really look down, though, otherwise I'll get sick."

"You and heights have never mixed even when you were a kid," said Dad. "I'm sure you'll get over it, however. Now you should try to land near me."

"Okay," I said. I gulped. "Can I do it *without* looking down?"

"Your aim would be off if you did that," said Dad. "Just do it slowly. No need to hurry."

"All right," I said. "I'm coming—hey, what's that?"

I heard what sounded like a jet approaching me. I looked around, but I didn't see any planes in the sky around me. All I saw was the blue sky, the sun, and the clouds beneath me, yet that jet engine sound was still clear.

"Kevin?" said Dad again. "What do you hear?"

"Something that sounds like a jet engine," I said, turning this way and that as I searched for it. "But I don't see any jets."

"Odd," Dad's voice crackled in my ear. "I picked this location to test your flight powers specifically because no commercial airlines fly here, which I thought would minimize the possibility of a plane flying into you."

The jet engine sound was much closer now than before, but I still couldn't see its source. I decided to try to land now before whatever it was hit me when something exploded out of a nearby cloud and surged toward me almost too fast for my eyes to follow.

THE SUPERHERO'S TEST

My reflexes, however, were as fast as ever. I flew to the side, narrowly avoiding the thing that was coming at me. I watched as the thing flew away from me, came to a stop, and then turned to face me.

It was a robot. It was bigger and taller than me, with thick steel plating that made me wonder how it was even remaining airborne. Flames shot out from its feet, which were apparently its exhaust ports. Its face was nothing more than a glowing red stripe with a voice box directly below it. It also had two guns for hands, which made me wonder how it was supposed to grab anything.

"What the hell?" I said. "Dad, what is that?"

"I'd like to help you, Kevin, but I can't see it very well from down here," said Dad's sardonic voice in my ear. "Can you describe whatever it is you see to me?"

"It's a robot," I said. "A flying robot."

"A flying robot?" said Dad. His voice became serious. "Uh oh."

"Uh oh?" I said. "Dad, do you know what that thing—"

I was interrupted when the robot aimed its hands at me and started firing off bullets. I dropped through the clouds, just barely avoiding getting riddled with bullets, and then shot through the air toward the robot. I tried to punch it, but the robot dodged, allowing me to fly straight past it.

"Kevin!" Dad's voice shouted in my ear. "I heard bullets being shot. Are you okay?"

"Yeah, but just barely," I said, looking over my shoulder at the robot, which was now following me. "What should I do? Should I go back to you?"

"No," said Dad. "Try to distract it. I'll see if I can get one of my drones to back you up."

"Distract it?" I said. "How?"

"Just do whatever you can," said Dad. "And whatever you do, remain calm and don't panic."

Remain calm? How was I supposed to remain calm with a flying killer robot coming after me? I was going to ask Dad that, but then I heard the sound of bullets coming at me and I twisted and turned, dodging most of them, although one bullet grazed my shoulder. It didn't hurt or even cut through my suit, but the impact of the bullet nonetheless sent me spiraling through the sky before I regained my balance and flew back into the air.

Looking over my shoulder again, I saw that the robot was still on my tail. I had never seen a robot like this before. It didn't look like anything Dad might have made. It looked like something from out of a video game, which made me wonder again where the hell it had come from.

But it didn't matter where it came from. What mattered was that I needed to destroy it before it destroyed me.

So I stopped, turned around, and flew toward it. This change of tactics seemed to take the robot by surprise, because it stopped in midair for a moment before raising its gun hands and aiming at me.

But I didn't give it a chance to fire a single bullet. I slammed into its abdomen with my shoulder, knocking the robot back and sending it falling to the earth below. I zipped after it, but then the robot started firing at me as it fell and I had to swerve to avoid getting hit again.

As I flew away, I looked back and saw that the robot had already recovered from the attack and was flying after me again.

Now, however, it looked less like a robot and more like a plane, with its arms and legs combining together to give it less wind resistance. What, was it a Transformer, too?

Then it started shooting at me again. I flew upwards sharply to avoid getting riddled with bullets, while the killer robot zipped by underneath. I floated in the sky for a moment, watching as the robot changed course to come after me again.

Again, it aimed its guns at me, but I didn't stay still long enough for it to take aim. Instead, I flew over and landed on its back, putting all of my weight on it in an attempt to make it fall to the ground. We actually did fall several feet before the plane transformed again, forcing me to jump off it just as it returned to its killer robot mode.

But rather than shoot me with its guns, a cannon rose off the robot's back and fired a missile at me. The missile soared through the air toward me, forcing me to fly as fast as I could to avoid it, but it must have been a heat-seeker, because it started following me just like the robot itself.

"Dad?" I said into my earcom, glancing over my shoulder at the missile that was following me. "Is the drone ready yet?"

"I'm working on it," said Dad. "And yes, I am aware of the missile following you."

"Great," I said, banking to the left in an attempt to lose the missile, although the missile kept following me. "So what do you think will happen if it hits me? Do you think I'll explode and discover that I have the power of regeneration?"

"Not sure," said Dad, who sounded like he was seriously considering the question. "Your powers are similar to Omega Man's, so there's a good chance you'll survive, although I can't say the same about your suit."

"Dad, that was just a joke," I said. "Anyway, talk to you later. I'm going to try to lose this missile."

I clicked my earcom off and increased my speed, but the missile was still on my tail. Actually, it seemed to be flying even faster than me, because it was getting closer and closer with every passing second. I figured that it would not be long before it actually caught up with me and blew me into chunks of meat, at which point I probably wouldn't need to worry about Master Chaos killing me anymore.

I needed to stop the robot. I figured that it probably had control of the missile, so if I could kill the bot, then I could stop the missile. It was worth a shot.

So I flew upwards sharply and then flew back the way I came, flying over the missile, which soon turned in midair and resumed following me. I looked around the sky for the robot until I spotted it hiding near some clouds, obviously trying to avoid being spotted by me.

I shot toward the robot. It noticed me immediately and started firing more bullets at me, but I avoided them easily. The missile was still following me, but that gave me an idea about how to get rid of both it and the robot at the same time.

I quickly flew upwards and then cut off my power, causing me to go backwards through the air until I was above the missile, which I landed on. Then I wrapped my arms and legs around the missile and flew it straight at the robot, which must have been surprised by my tactic, because it didn't even move as the missile drew closer and closer to it.

At the last second, I let go of the missile and flew off as fast as I could. I managed to get several hundred feet away from the cloud before the missile collided with the bot and exploded, creating a massive explosion, the shock wave from it sending me hurtling through the air. I spun through the air crazily for a couple of seconds before regaining my balance and looking over my shoulder, wondering if the missile had destroyed the robot.

I didn't see the robot anymore. All I saw was a bare patch of sky where a bunch of clouds had been, clouds that had been vaporized by the explosion. The robot must have been vaporized, too, because I didn't see anything to indicate that it had ever been there.

I activated my earcom again and said, "Dad! I managed to blow up the robot. Did you see?"

"I saw the explosion," Dad's voice crackled in my ear. "But I didn't see the debris of the robot fall. Are you sure you destroyed it?"

"Yeah!" I said. "It totally vaporized the clouds. I bet that the robot was also—"

The sound of a loud jet engine interrupted me, causing me to look over my shoulder just in time to see that same robot—now blackened from the fire of the explosion—hurtling toward me from the clouds. I didn't have time to dodge. The robot slammed into my back, sending me flying uncontrollably through the air. I heard Dad yelling in my ear, but I was too disoriented to respond.

In fact, now I was falling, falling through the sky toward the ground. The impact of the robot's blow made it hard for me to regain control. The sky and ground kept switching places as I fell, but I managed to regain control of my powers quickly and started flying again.

But then the robot came out of nowhere and tackled me like a football player. I tried to wrestle out of its grasp, but the robot wouldn't let go. We just fell and fell through the sky, wrestling for dominance, until we crashed into the earth. The impact dazed me, but the robot was already recovering. It stood up and slammed its foot down on top of me, knocking the breath out of my lungs. Then it aimed one of its gun hands at me and I knew my life was over, because I couldn't move in time to dodge the bullet.

Then, all of a sudden, I heard the sound of helicopter blades slashing through the air and in the next instant a small, white-colored drone flew out of nowhere. It fired a dozen bullets at the robot, causing the killer robot to look at the drone. The robot was distracted only for a moment, but it was long enough for me to regain my strength.

I shoved the robot's foot off of me, making it stagger backwards. Before the robot could recover from that, I jumped to my feet and punched it as hard as I could through its stomach. My hand smashed through steel plating, wiring, and everything else inside the robot, making it fall over with a crash. But it still tried to get up, so I jumped into the air, using my flying powers to give me an extra boost, and then fell straight down on its head.

My feet crashed through the robot's skull, smashing it to pieces. The robot's body immediately went still, which was how I knew that it was down for good.

Stepping off of the remains of the robot's head, I looked at the drone, which was floating nearby, though it had retracted its gun. The drone had the same white color as most of Dad's equipment, so I figured that the drone must have been created by Dad.

Just as I thought that, Dad himself appeared next to me

seemingly out of nowhere, although he appeared to have teleported, teleported because he took his hand off the Teleportation Buckle as soon as he appeared next to me.

"Kevin, are you all right?" said Dad, looking down at me.

I looked down at my suit. It was muddy and soggy, probably from the impact of the fall. I felt my hair, which was also quite dirty, but I didn't feel any blood or anything. My body ached from the impact, though nothing felt broken, which surprised me, given how hard and far I had fallen. Guess I must have been even stronger than I thought.

Lowering my hands to my side, I said, "I'm okay. But what is that robot? Where did it come from?"

I gestured at the headless robot beside me, which Dad immediately walked over toward. Bending over the robot, Dad looked its body up and down, but his Genius helmet made it impossible for me to tell what he was thinking. I could tell that he was at least as troubled about the robot as I was, if not more so, which made me think that he had to have an idea about its nature and origin.

"I've never seen this kind of robot before," said Dad as he stood up. He sounded troubled. "It looks like it was designed for war."

"War?" I said. "You mean like a military weapon?"

"Possibly," said Dad. "That would explain its gun hands and the missile launcher on its back."

I looked at the robot again. I wondered what a military robot was doing all the way out here in Texas when a sudden, terrible theory occurred to me.

I looked at Dad and said, "Dad, do you think this is one of the top-secret military weapons that Master Chaos stole from the military?"

"I think it very likely," said Dad. "I'll need to contact the G-Men about this and let them know that we've found one of their weapons."

Dad didn't sound very excited about that, which made sense, because Dad never seemed very excited about talking to the government about anything.

"Good idea, but this still freaks me out," I said. I looked up at the sky, but didn't see any other killer robots raining death from above. "But if that's what this robot is, then does that mean that Master Chaos knows my secret identity? Did he send it to kill me so he wouldn't have to do it himself? How did it even know where to find us, anyway?"

"I don't know," said Dad. "It's possible Master Chaos simply wants to eliminate any neoheroes in Silvers to make it easier for him to get us. Because you are the only known neohero in town, that makes you a prime target, though that still doesn't explain how he knew where we were training."

"Is Master Chaos watching us?" I said anxiously.

"I don't know," said Dad. "What we need to do is contact the G-Men and inform them about what we found so they can take it away and possibly use it to find out where Chaos is."

"Are we still going to continue my training, then?" I said.

"Not today," said Dad, shaking his head. "I don't want to put you in anymore danger, not if Master Chaos knows where we are. Let's go home for now and wait until we hear back from the government. Seeker One, my drone, will keep an eye on the robot's remains until someone from the government comes to pick

THE SUPERHERO'S TEST

them up."

CHAPTER FIFTEEN

WHEN WE RETURNED HOME, Dad immediately went down into the Lab to contact the government, while I returned to my room to rest and relax. But first, I explained to Mom why we had returned from training so early. I tried to make the fact that a flying killer robot had tried to kill me sound not quite as bad as it was, but Mom was still worried by the time I finished explaining it to her and she was in no mood to listen to my constant reassurances that I was okay and hadn't been badly hurt. I did, however, let her wash my super suit, mostly because it was really dirty and smelled bad and needed the wash.

For the next couple of hours, the atmosphere in our house was very tense. I fully expected Master Chaos to show up at any moment and kick down our front door, or for more of those government robots to fly over our house and blow it up with missiles. Dad didn't seem that worried; at least I didn't think he was, considering how he did not come out of his Lab with any bad news.

I tried to pass the time by playing games on my phone, but I found it hard to focus on them because I was so worried about Master Chaos. Almost getting killed by his robot had completely changed the way I looked at Master Chaos. His threat—both to my life and to my family's safety—suddenly seemed a lot more real than it had just a few hours ago. I wasn't sure how to take it. I normally wasn't one to stress over things, but this was different because my safety, and the safety of my family, was at risk.

After what seemed like forever, I heard a knock at my door. Sitting up in my bed, I said, "Who is it?"

"It's me," said Dad's voice from the other side of the door. "Can I come in? I have some updates for you."

"All right," I said. "Let yourself in."

The door opened and Dad stepped inside. He was no longer wearing his Genius costume or helmet, thus revealing his worried face, which made him look older than he really was. He closed the door behind him, but did not come closer to my bed.

"So?" I said. "What's the news?"

"I contacted the NHA, who said they would deliver this information to the G-Men," said Dad. "I was told that the government will probably send someone to pick up the robot's remains later today and haul them to whatever secret facility the government has."

"Did you learn anything about what the robot was?" I said. "Like, what kind of weapon it's supposed to be?"

Dad sighed and rubbed his forehead. "I don't know much about it, but when Master Chaos stole those weapons from that facility, the government did share a few details about the weapons with the NHA, who then shared it with me so I'd know what Master Chaos might send after us."

"What kind of details?" I said.

"Well, the weapons are part of a top-secret government project known as Project Neo," said Dad. "They're supposed to be the next generation of high-tech military weaponry, including

159

some of the first humanoid robots designed to be deployed onto a battlefield during war. I don't know the exact number of weapons Master Chaos managed to steal, but I do know that he stole a lot."

"Project Neo?" I said. "Will the government be able to use the remains of the robot we destroyed to track down Master Chaos?"

"Possibly, but I doubt it," said Dad. "Chaos may have programmed the robot to go after you, but I am under the impression, based on what I've been told, that the robot doesn't record the location of its programmer in its coding. Regardless, this doesn't change the fact that Master Chaos will likely send more of these things after you soon."

"Then what am I supposed to do?" I said. "Hide and hope he doesn't get us?"

Dad shook his head, pushing his glasses back up the bridge of his nose. "No. We need to continue your training no matter what Master Chaos does. But I have to admit that this is starting to look grim. I can only imagine that this must be part of Chaos's plan, a plan I wish I understood better."

"Do you think he knows our secret identities?" I said. "Because if he does—"

"Unlikely," said Dad, interrupting me. "As I said earlier, I think it far more likely that he wants to ensure there are no neoheroes in Silvers who can stop him from harming us. Or maybe he was testing out the robot to see how it worked in actual combat."

"Well, it obviously didn't work very well," I said, "considering how easily we defeated it."

"Maybe, but one fact I know about Chaos is that, unlike other villains, he doesn't do the same thing over and over when it's shown to fail the first time," said Dad. "No doubt he'll try something even more sinister later, though what, I cannot say, because he is very unpredictable."

"Wait, what if he shows up here while we're out training and attacks Mom?" I said. "She can't defend herself. She doesn't have powers like us."

"Valerie has been defending the house while we've been out," said Dad. "Remember, I have her hooked up to the house's security system. She scans any and all people who come to or near the house to ensure that they aren't threats. If Master Chaos should ever come up to our front door while we're away, Valerie should keep him busy long enough for us to return and beat him ourselves."

I was doubtful that Valerie could hold off someone like Master Chaos for very long, but Dad seemed confident that she could, so I didn't push the question any further.

Instead, I said, "So will the NHA be sending people to help us? Because if Master Chaos is so close by, then don't you think we should get some backup?"

"It wouldn't surprise me if the NHA does send some members to search the nearest towns and cities for Master Chaos," said Dad. "And I expect the G-Men to do the same, because they're also on the case. It may be inevitable at this point, especially if Master Chaos is as close as we think."

"Does this mean I won't be able to go back to school anymore?" I said. "Is school still safe?"

"I believe so, but we'll need to take extra precautions," said Dad. "Master Chaos is unpredictable, but if he is willing to attack us so brazenly like that, then I doubt he'll hesitate to attack a high school full of innocent kids who don't have any super powers of their own."

"Maybe I shouldn't go to school at all, then," I said. "I don't want to put anyone else's life at risk because of me."

"I understand what you mean, but I think staying home would not be a wise decision," said Dad. "You still need to pursue your education, regardless of what Master Chaos chooses to do. I will speak with the NHA and the government about ways in which we might keep your school safe."

My shoulders slumped. I had hoped that Dad would agree that I shouldn't go to school, but I guess I should have seen that answer coming. I lay back down on my bed and sighed.

"So, will we be resuming my training later or tomorrow?" I said.

"I don't think we'll be doing any more training for the rest of the weekend," said Dad. "I need to consult with the NHA and the G-Men about this recent turn of events. But I don't want you to leave the house until Monday when you have to go to school."

I sighed, but said, "Okay, I won't. What am I going to do until then?"

"Whatever you want," said Dad, who didn't sound very concerned about it. "Just try to enjoy the weekend, like a normal teenage boy."

"Normal?" I said, looking up at Dad in disbelief. "Dad, how many normal teenage boys have super powers?"

"You know what I mean," said Dad. "Anyway, I need to leave and speak with the NHA and G-Men about this again. Mom wanted me to let you know that dinner will be ready soon."

With that, Dad left my room, closing the door behind him on

the way out.

I didn't move from my position on my bed. I just stared up at the ceiling, feeling so frustrated and helpless. I had thought that moving to Texas was going to be boring, but it felt like I had never had a moment of boredom since arriving. And I wasn't sure I liked that, because safe boredom seemed better than the constant stress that seemed to follow me wherever I went.

I was getting tired of this. Tired of Master Chaos playing us in the shadows, never knowing when he was going to strike. I hated feeling like a scared little kid. And I knew this feeling would never leave me as long as Master Chaos was out there plotting my demise.

Yeah, I knew the NHA and the G-Men were on it, but what had they done so far to stop Chaos? Not much, as far as I could tell. Chaos had even stolen some secret military weapons right from under the government's nose, for Pete's sake. How could I rely on the NHA or the G-Men to protect me if they couldn't even prevent a simple theft like that?

It was obvious that something had to be done. Master Chaos needed to be stopped. And it wasn't the NHA or the G-Men who would stop him.

If Master Chaos wanted me, then he was going to get me … but on my terms. And I was already thinking of a plan that would allow me to find him, whether or not Dad or anyone else approved.

CHAPTER SIXTEEN

I SPENT PRETTY MUCH the whole weekend cooped up in my room, thinking about my plan and figuring it all out. I didn't come out very much except to use the bathroom or get meals. Neither Mom nor Dad asked me about what I was doing, but that was fine, because I didn't want to share my plan with them, not when I knew that they wouldn't support it. After all, they had been doing everything within their power to keep me *away* from Master Chaos, whereas I was already planning to confront him myself.

I didn't know where Master Chaos was. For all I knew, he could be on the other side of the country or maybe even on the other side of the world. But I knew he was after me and I knew that if I went after him, sooner or later I *would* find him, and once I did, we would fight and one of us—and only one of us—would survive.

But I couldn't put my plan into action right away. I needed help. I couldn't go to Mom or Dad for help for obvious reasons, but I knew someone who would be willing to help me. I even sent him a text message on Sunday, telling him to meet me after school on Monday so we could talk about it.

That someone was Malcolm, who agreed to meet me after school. I didn't tell him the details about what I wanted to talk with him. I just told him that I had something very important to tell him, a secret that he would not be allowed to share with anyone else. Malcolm seemed really interested in my secret, but he didn't bug me about it. He just said that he couldn't wait until after school for us to hang out, because we hadn't actually hung out after school since I arrived in Silvers. I didn't invite Tara, for obvious reasons.

But it turned out that we might have to postpone the meeting for a while, because as I walked up to John Smith High School, I saw a couple of people standing on either side of the entrance who I had never seen before. One was a tall, muscular black guy whose skin looked like literal oil, with a few fancy golden rings around his fingers, while the other was a white guy with a huge, rhinoceros-like metal horn jutting out of his forehead. Both of them wore an identical black uniform with a bald eagle head patch on their right shoulders, although I didn't recommend the patch.

They looked like police men or Secret Service guys, but there was no way that the President of the United States was here. I stopped on the sidewalk and watched as other students entering the school walked by them. Some of the students stared at the two large men, while others just kept their heads down or looked straight ahead. I didn't blame them. Those two guys looked like they could crack concrete with their bare hands, or, in the case of the horned guy, with that huge metal horn on his head.

"Kevin!" said a voice behind me, causing me to look over my shoulder and see Malcolm, with his backpack slung over his shoulder, walking up to me.

"Hey, Mal," I said as Malcolm stopped next to me. I looked at the two men at the entrance to the school, who had their hands folded behind their backs and had not uttered a word so far. "Who are those guys?"

"Oh, they're with the G-Men," said Malcolm. "You know, the government-sponsored superhero team?"

"Yeah, I guessed that already," I said. "But who are they, exactly? And why are there two G-Men here in Silvers, of all places?"

"The guy with the oily skin is Black Gold," said Malcolm, pointing at the muscular black guy I had noticed earlier. "He can turn into and control oil." Then he pointed at the horned guy. "And that's Iron Horn. See that horn on his head? It's actually a metal covering, protecting the huge horn that grew out of his skull from harm. He's one of the physically strongest neoheroes in the world and even went toe-to-toe with Omega Man once and almost won."

"Really?" I said. I glanced at Black Gold and Iron Horn, whose attention seemed more focused on the sky than on the street before them. "I thought the G-Men were just a bunch of losers."

"Yeah, they're not as cool as the Neohero Alliance, but they've still got some pretty cool guys on their team," said Malcolm. "Though I'd watch what you say to Iron Horn there. His Neo Ranks page says he has a really bad temper and doesn't take well to jokes made at his expense."

I could believe that. While both of the two G-Men agents looked tough and unfriendly, I could at least see Black Gold cracking a joke. Iron Horn, on the other hand, looked like he was in a perpetually bad mood, like he had woken up on the wrong side of the bed every morning.

"So what are they doing here?" I said, looking at Malcolm again. "I don't remember Principal Thomas telling us that we'd have a couple of G-Men guarding the school today."

"I heard about it from my older brother," said Malcolm. "He works under Cadmus Smith, the Director of the G-Men. Said that the government is worried that Master Chaos might attack our school, so they sent a couple of their agents to protect it."

That puzzled me until I remembered that Dad said that the government was likely going to do something about the fact that Master Chaos had sent that robot to try to kill us. I hadn't realized they'd send these two agents so soon, however. I thought we wouldn't see a response from the government for a while.

"Why do they think Master Chaos might attack our school?" I said, looking at Malcolm again.

"Because they think Master Chaos wants to kill one of the students here," said Malcolm. "Remember Robert Candle? He's actually Master Chaos's son. Crazy, right?"

"But Robert was harmed by an air bomb," I said. "An air bomb he made. Why would Master Chaos think that any of the students here had anything to do with harming Robert?"

"I don't know, but that's the current theory," said Malcolm. "Anyway, Master Chaos is supposed to be crazy. He probably doesn't even know what he's doing. I heard he was a patient in a mental asylum before he got his powers, so he's probably suffering from some kind of mental illness or something."

I didn't consider that very likely. If Dad was telling the truth, then Master Chaos knew exactly what he was doing, even if he did have some kind of mental illness.

But I didn't say that out loud. I said, "Is that all?"

"Well, I also heard on Neo Ranks that one of the top government secret weapons that Master Chaos stole was seen near town," said Malcolm. "Allegedly, it attacked Bolt, though he defeated it. You know, that new hero who lives right here in good old Silvers?"

I had to hide my surprise at Malcolm's knowledge of my recent encounter with one of Master Chaos's robots. "Where did you hear about that?"

"Like I said, on Neo Ranks," said Malcolm. "I was just reading the Rumors board and someone claimed to have witnessed a battle between Bolt and a transforming robot a couple of hours outside of town. I don't know anything else about it, though."

Witness? That didn't make any sense. Dad and I were alone when we were training. Sure, I did blow up the robot, which likely would have drawn the attention of anyone nearby, but Dad had specifically picked out a training area that didn't have any people in it. Either that person on Neo Ranks was lying and had somehow learned about my encounter with the robot somewhere else or Dad was secretly talking about our training sessions online, which hardly seemed likely to me, though the first explanation didn't make any sense, either.

Whatever the case, I wasn't sure what to make of this. Sure, having two neoheroes protecting the school from Master Chaos made sense, especially if Iron Horn really was as strong as Omega Man, but I also felt worried. If the government thought we needed two powerful neoheroes protecting the school, then that meant that they thought it was very likely that Master Chaos was going to attack the school sometime soon. I didn't see any sign of Master Chaos nearby; nonetheless, I felt nervous, because I knew that any clash between Master Chaos and the G-Men wouldn't be pretty.

It also made me rethink my plan. I was originally planning to slip out of school today and go flying around the country in search of Master Chaos, but if these two G-Men were here, then I likely wouldn't be able to do that. And if I tried, they'd probably just catch me and bring me back to school.

Nonetheless, I was determined to get that confrontation with Master Chaos one way or another, so I said, "Well, I'm glad that we've got two powerful neoheroes protecting us."

"Yeah, it's cool," said Malcolm, nodding excitedly. "While the G-Men aren't as cool as the NHA, I still think they're pretty awesome. After all, how often do you see real life superheroes in Silvers? Not very often, I think."

"Right," I said. "Anyway, we should go inside. School's about to start."

"Oh, yeah," said Malcolm. Then he frowned. "By the way, what did you want to talk with me about after school? I mean, you don't have to tell me now if you don't want to, but if you could give me a heads up, I'd appreciate it."

I looked at my suit-up watch, which also happened to double as an actual watch. "Looks like we have some time before our first class." I looked up at Malcolm again. "Let's go inside and find a private place to talk. It shouldn't take us very long, so we should be done in a few minutes at most."

"Well, I hope so," said Malcolm as he and I started walking toward the school's entrance, "because I've been late to Mrs.

Tanner's class too many times this week and she's not going to be happy if I'm late again."

"Why are you late to Mrs. Tanner's class?" I said, tilting my head to the side. "Don't you live close to the school?"

"Eh, just home problems," said Malcolm. His tone made it clear that I wasn't supposed to ask him what that meant, so I didn't.

We walked past Black Gold and Iron Horn. I tried not to look suspicious and I don't think either of them paid me or Malcolm any more attention than they did to the other students entering. Still, I worried that they might somehow be able to sense the presence of a nearby neohero and that they might reveal my secret identity here and now, although I knew that was silly, because neoheroes couldn't sense each other like that.

When Malcolm and I got into the crowded hallway of the school, I led him to the boy's bathroom. Once we were inside, I locked the door and turned to face Malcolm, who was now looking at me impatiently.

"So? What did you want to talk with me about?" said Malcolm.

I didn't answer right away. I walked past him, checking each stall, just to make sure there wasn't anyone in here with us. Every stall was empty, so I turned around to face Malcolm again.

"All right," I said. "What I am about to show you will probably blow your mind, so you have to promise me not to scream. Okay?"

"Um, okay," said Malcolm, although he sounded really hesitant. "You don't have a dead animal or something in your backpack, do you?"

THE SUPERHERO'S TEST

"Of course not," I said. I dropped my backpack on the ground. "But you're sure you won't freak out?"

"Absolutely," said Malcolm. "I am a very calm person. I never freak out over anything. When you come from a family as large as mine, you kind of get used to seeing freaky things."

"All right," I said. "Here we go."

I pressed the button on my suit-up watch. The screen flipped open, my suit shot out, and I was suddenly dressed from head to toe in my super suit.

I looked at Malcolm again. His mouth hung open and he was staring at me like he had just been electrocuted. In fact, I was almost convinced that he had died right there and then, which would have been really hard to explain to Dad if he found out.

"What …" Malcolm seemed to have lost the ability to speak. "What … Huh? … Um …"

"Your eyes aren't deceiving you," I said. I patted my chest. "This suit is the real deal. It's not some kind of fancy cosplay or anything."

"No way …" Malcolm shook his head. "Nah, man. This has got to be a joke. Did you and Tara get together to make me think that you're Bolt?"

"No, I really am Bolt," I said. "This isn't some kind of joke. Besides, you know that Tara would never have gone along with a joke like this, if it was one. She hates neoheroes so much that she'd probably punch me if I suggested this plan to her."

"Right," said Malcolm, who didn't sound entirely convinced. "Well, I don't see any proof that you're Bolt, aside from that convincing-looking suit you're wearing, but it could just be a replica you bought from a store or something."

I sighed and, focusing on my flight powers, hovered a few inches off the floor. It was a very gentle movement, but Malcolm stumbled backwards, almost falling onto his behind. He stared at me in horror, like I had just transformed into some kind of monster.

I gestured at my suit again. "Is this proof enough? Or should I lift the entire school above my head?"

"Okay, man, okay," said Malcolm, holding up his hands like he was afraid that I was going to punch him through the bathroom wall. "I believe you. Can you stop floating like that? It's creepy."

I raised an eyebrow as I landed on the bathroom floor. "Creepy? I thought you were going to say it's cool."

"Cool?" said Malcolm. "Look, if you weren't, well, you, then I might think it's cool, but knowing that my best friend is a neohero ... I dunno, man. It's weird."

"Well, it's also true," I said. "But I won't use my powers around you right now if it will freak you out like that."

"Thanks, man," said Malcolm. Then he looked at me with more curiosity. "How long have you been a neohero? When did you get your powers?"

"I—" I began, before Malcolm interrupted me by whipping out his smartphone and saying, "Hold on. I need to get your Neo Ranks page up so I can include this information in your bio."

I dashed over to Malcolm before he could open the Neo Ranks app, however, and snatched his phone out of his hand, holding it just outside of his reach as I stepped away from him.

"Hey!" Malcolm protested. "That's my phone! Give it back."

"Not if you're going to be putting up all my secrets on Neo Ranks," I said, shaking my head. "I'm technically not supposed to be revealing my secret identity to *anyone*. I'm just revealing it to you because I think you deserve to know, because you're the only person outside of my family I trust with this information."

Malcolm lowered his hands. "Okay. I won't post anything about Bolt that you tell me on your Neo Ranks page. Now can I please have my phone back?"

Sensing that Malcolm was telling the truth, I handed him back his phone, which he put into the pocket of his jeans. Then he looked at me again and said, "All right. I'm ready to listen to your story."

"Okay," I said. "I'll try to be quick so we're not late for class."

As quickly and briefly as I could, I explained my origin, where I got my suit from, who my dad was, and everything else I thought Malcolm needed to know. Malcolm listened, his expression becoming more and more excited the more I told him. I didn't understand what he was so excited about, but I didn't ask him about it until I finished.

"And that is why the G-Men are protecting the school," I finished. "Master Chaos is after me. Or really, he's after Kevin Jason, though he doesn't like Bolt, either."

Malcolm looked like he was trying to process everything I had told him. I expected him to start asking me some pretty serious questions, like what I thought Master Chaos was planning or if I felt prepared to risk my life to fight him.

Instead, however, Malcolm said, "Your Dad's *the* Genius? One of the Four Founders? That's badass. Can I get his autograph?"

"What?" I said. "Is that your biggest concern? Aren't you worried that your best friend is on the hit list of one of the world's worst supervillains?"

"Yeah, sure, that's serious, but my other question still stands," said Malcolm. He rubbed his hands together eagerly. "Oh, man. This is awesome. I'm best friends with the son of one of the most famous superheroes in the world. And here I thought you were just a kid from New York."

I was starting to rethink my decision to share my secret identity with Malcolm, but I supposed it was too late now and anyway Dad wouldn't trust me with the Memory Hacker.

"Well, I'm glad you're supportive, at least," I said. "But it doesn't matter whose son I am. What matters is that Master Chaos is after me. That's why Black Gold and Iron Horn are protecting the school."

Malcolm's eager grin suddenly vanished, replaced by an anxious frown. "Holy cow. You mean Master Chaos is after *you* specifically?"

"Yeah, I just said that," I said, feeling annoyed that Malcolm apparently hadn't been listening as closely as I thought. "But I'm not going to wait until Master Chaos comes knocking at my front door or attacks the school. I'm going to search for him and fight him on my own terms."

Malcolm's face turned pale. "You're going after Master Chaos? Why? Do you want to get yourself killed or something?"

"I'm not suicidal," I said, shaking my head. "I'm just tired of living in fear of Master Chaos attacking me or my family or friends. I don't want to risk your lives just to keep myself 'safe.'"

"You sound like a real neohero, you know that?" said Malcolm. "Like Omega Man, actually."

"Well, I'm just doing what's right," I said with a shrug. "I figure if I can track down Master Chaos myself and fight him on my own terms, then I can limit the amount of collateral damage a fight between us would likely cause."

"So do you know where he is?" said Malcolm. "'Cause both the NHA and the G-Men have been searching for him and still haven't found a clue to his location."

"No, but I know that Master Chaos is after me," I said. "If I search for him, he'll probably come to me or reveal himself at some point. Remember, Master Chaos wants me dead, so I don't think I'll have to work hard to find him."

"Okay, but how are you going to leave?" said Malcolm. "What about your schoolwork? Have you told your parents what you're planning to do?"

I looked down at my feet sheepishly. "Well, no, I haven't. My parents would never approve of me hunting down Master Chaos on my own. Dad doesn't think I'm ready to face him yet. He just wants me to let the NHA and the G-Men handle it and only to fight Master Chaos if I have no other option left. I think Dad is wrong, but I know I won't be able to convince him of that, so I didn't tell him what I'm going to do."

"I think your dad might be right," said Malcolm. "I heard that one time Master Chaos fought Omega Man, the Midnight Menace, and Lady Amazon all by himself and actually fought them to a draw. Those guys are some of the strongest and most experienced neoheroes in the world, so I don't know how well you'd stand against him in a fight."

"I know," I said. "I don't look forward to fighting him, but I must. I'm tired of hiding from him and hoping that the NHA and the G-Men stop him before he harms me or someone I care about.

I want to be proactive."

"If you say so," said Malcolm with a shrug. "Listen, man, I'll support and pray for you whatever you choose to do. If you think that you need to do this to save your family and friends, then I'll help however I can."

I smiled. "Thanks, Mal. I knew I could count on you."

"Besides, you're the first neohero I actually know," said Malcolm. He rubbed his hands together eagerly. "Man, I'd love to be able to go onto Neo Ranks and brag that I'm friends with a *real* neohero. Everyone else will be so jealous."

"Let's focus on what's important at the moment," I said. "First things first: I need your help to get out of the school without anyone noticing."

"My help?" said Malcolm. "How am I supposed to help? Do you want me to tell Mrs. Tanner that you got sick and had to go home?"

"No," I said. "Well, I mean, that's one excuse, but I'd need to get a note from one of my parents excusing me from school if I pretended to be sick and I don't have time to do that. I really just need help distracting Black Gold and Iron Horn."

"Why would they stop you?" said Malcolm.

"Because I'm not supposed to be going after Master Chaos," I said. "If they see me trying to leave, they'll try to stop me. I need you to distract them so I can get away. It doesn't need to be for long; I can fly very fast, so by the time they figure out what you're doing, I should be long gone."

Malcolm gulped. "What if they get angry at me? They're neoheroes, after all."

"I doubt they'll harm you," I said. "After all, you're not doing anything illegal or harmful. You might get in trouble with the school, though."

Malcolm ran his hands through his short hair, looking disturbed. "And my older brother really wouldn't be happy if he learned I got in the way of some of his colleagues. Nor would my parents, for that matter."

"I know, but I need a distraction if I am going to get out of here and stop Master Chaos," I said. "Can I count on you to do it? I know you are already in a lot of trouble with the school for other things you've done, but you said you would help me no matter what."

"Yeah, I did," said Malcolm. "All right, bro, I'll help you. Even if it gets me expelled from the school, I'd like to be able to tell everyone that I helped the famous Bolt defeat Master Chaos."

"Famous?" I said. "I'm not famous, except maybe here in Silvers."

"Yeah, but you *will* be famous after you defeat Master Chaos all by yourself," said Malcolm, patting me on the shoulder with a large grin on his face. "Maybe you'll even be as famous as Omega Man."

I briefly imagined myself flying down to some city somewhere, landing in the streets, and being mobbed by hundreds of fans (mostly hot girls). It distracted me for a moment before I shook my head and focused on the situation again.

"Yeah, that would be awesome, but that's not important," I said. "Right now, I need to focus on getting out of the school without being caught."

"Like I said, man, I'll help you in whatever ways I can," said Malcolm. "So what's the plan?"

I glanced at my suit-up watch to see the time. "Okay. We don't have much time, so I'll keep it quick. Here's the plan."

CHAPTER SEVENTEEN

WHEN I FINISHED TELLING Malcolm the plan, we had to go to class because we didn't want to be late. We were going to attempt to get me out of the school at lunchtime, which I figured would be the best time to attempt to leave the campus due to the fact that everyone would be in the cafeteria, which would lessen the chance of a teacher or someone else catching us. I would have left right away, but Malcolm said that he didn't want to miss any of his first period classes.

It was hard to wait, though, because I really wanted to leave right away. I kept looking either at my watch or at the clocks on the walls of our classrooms, but it seemed like time had been broken, because their arms never seemed to move. I barely paid attention in class (which earned me more than a few criticisms from my teachers) because I spent almost all of my time thinking about my upcoming confrontation with Master Chaos.

When lunchtime finally came, Malcolm and I went to the cafeteria with everyone else, because it would look suspicious if we didn't. We even went as far as to pick out our lunch and sit at our usual table, although this time Tara was already there before we were. As usual, she didn't seem to be paying much attention to us. I almost considered letting her in on the plan at the last minute, but I decided against it; she was so anti-neohero that I figured she would be more of a liability than a help. Besides, it was too late to involve anyone else in the plan at this point.

So Malcolm and I sat down at the table, but Tara, as usual, didn't even greet us. She was just swiping through what looked like her Instagram account, looking through pictures, but I couldn't tell what she was looking at, nor did I care.

"Hi, Tara," I said. "How was your weekend?"

"Average," said Tara, without looking at me. I noticed a hint of anger in her voice for some reason. "Yours?"

"Uh, pretty good," I said. I hesitated and then said, "You seem a bit angry."

For once, Tara looked at me, unimpressed. "Oh? What makes you think that?"

"Just your tone," I said.

"Well, that was awfully perceptive of you," said Tara, looking at her phone again. "I thought you'd have guessed why I was angry, too, but I guess your powers of perception don't go that far."

I glanced at Malcolm, who just shrugged like he was saying *I don't know, man. Girls, am I right?*

I looked at Tara again. "Um … is it because you didn't get enough sleep last night?'

"No," said Tara. "It's because of those two super jerks in the front of the school, Oil Face and Colonel Pokey or whatever their names are."

"Oh," I said. I felt like an idiot for not realizing that she was angry about the fact that two neoheroes were protecting the school. "Well, they're just here to protect the school from Master Chaos."

THE SUPERHERO'S TEST

"I still don't like them," said Tara. "They're freaks and probably perverts, too, or at least the guy with the horn on his head is. All those neo freaks are the same to me."

I looked at Malcolm again. I tried to non-verbally communicate *Time to go.*

Thankfully, Malcolm seemed to understand, because he stood up and said, in the least convincing voice I had ever heard in my life, "Well, gee whiz, guys, it looks like I really need to use the restroom. Do either of you wish to join me?"

Tara looked up at Malcolm like she thought he was an idiot. "Malcolm, I'm a girl. We use different bathrooms."

"Ah, but I am not," I said as I stood up. "Because you see, Tara, I am a boy and I also need to use the restroom. The boys' restroom, that is. Because I am a boy."

Tara looked from me to Malcolm with the most confusion I'd ever seen on her face. Then she shook her head and said, "Whatever. I'll make sure that Robert's friends don't take your lunch while you're away."

"That is awfully kind of you, Tara," said Malcolm, his voice still really fake. "Truly, you are a wonderful friend to Kevin and I."

"Indeed she is," I said, nodding. "Now, Malcolm, let us go to the boys' restroom, which is where we need to go. Because we are boys."

Tara didn't look at either of us as we left, but I had the distinct impression that she thought we were both idiots. And I felt like an idiot, but I didn't say anything about it until we left the cafeteria and were walking alone through the school's hallways.

Then I looked at Malcolm and said, "What the heck was

that?"

"What?" said Malcolm, looking at me. "I was just trying to make sure Tara didn't suspect us of doing anything we aren't supposed to do."

"By talking like an idiot?" I said as we turned down a corner. "Seriously, you could have just said, 'I need to use the bathroom' and I could said, 'Hey, me too. I'll go with you.'"

"If you thought that, then why did you go along with my way of doing things?" said Malcolm.

I shook my head. "Never mind. As long as no one follows us or suspect us of being up to something, then I guess it doesn't matter. Still, you could have at least acted a little less suspicious."

"Hey, I'm not an actor," said Malcolm, folding his arms over his chest. "If you wanted me to act differently, maybe you should have told me in the bathroom."

I rolled my eyes. "Whatever. We're out of the cafeteria now, so you know what the next step of the plan is."

Malcolm nodded. "Right. I distract Black Gold and Iron Horn while you slip away unseen for your big fight with Master Chaos."

"Good," I said. "So we'll need to split up. I'm going to head for the school's roof, where I will don my costume and fly away, while you go to the front of the school and distract the G-Men."

"Okay," said Malcolm. "But what will happen when everyone notices you are missing? What should I tell Tara or the teachers?"

"Tell them I got really sick from the cafeteria food and had to go home without telling anyone," I said. "Tell them you don't know when I'll be back in school but not to worry about me and that I will be back soon."

THE SUPERHERO'S TEST

"Okay," said Malcolm, though he sounded doubtful about that. "So I guess this is where we part, then."

We stopped in front of the school's trophy case. To the right, at the end of the hall, was the school's entrance, a set of glass doors through which I could see Black Gold and Iron Horn, who had their backs to the doors. To the left was another hall, which I knew would eventually lead me to a set of stairs that would take me to the school's roof.

I looked at Malcolm. "Yeah, this is where we'll split up."

"Okay," said Malcolm. "Do you know when you'll come back to school?"

I shook my head again. "No idea. It all depends on how quickly I find Master Chaos. I don't think he should be hard to find, but you never know. He's been in hiding from the NHA and the G-Men for weeks now and they still aren't any closer to finding him than when he first broke out."

"But he'll come after you," said Malcolm. "Can you beat him?"

I shrugged. "I don't know. I'm going to try my best, but it is possible Master Chaos could kill me, so this might be the last time we see each other."

"Well, I'll be praying for you, then, Kev," said Malcolm. He grasped my hand and we shook. "See you later and good luck with taking him down once and for all."

I nodded in return. Then I ran down the left hall, without looking back at Malcolm, because I didn't want to let any second thoughts keeping me from doing what I needed to do.

-

I reached the roof of the school without any trouble, although the door was locked with a thick padlock, which immediately snapped from one quick blow from my fist. Opening the door, I stepped out onto the roof and looked around quickly, just to make sure that I was actually alone. I didn't see any G-Men nearby, so I carefully walked over to the edge of the roof and peered over at the entrance below.

Black Gold and Iron Horn still stood there, their arms folded behind their backs and their eyes fixed on the street in front of the school. They were talking to each other, something about last night's football game or something. Neither of them seemed to notice or hear me moving along the rooftop, but I pulled away from the edge anyway and sat down to make sure they couldn't see me.

I pulled out my phone and quickly texted Malcolm a short message: *I'm on the roof. Start.*

I received a short message back: *All right.*

Then I heard the doors of the school open and, glancing over the edge of the roof, I saw Malcolm walk out of the school. But neither Black Gold nor Iron Horn paid him any attention until he walked quite intentionally into Iron Horn, causing Iron Horn to whirl around, raising his fists like he thought he was under attack.

Black Gold caught Iron Horn's arm before he could smash Malcolm into pieces and said, "Whoa, Captain, watch out! He's one of the students here. Looked like he walked into you by accident. No need to turn him into paste."

Iron Horn relaxed, lowering his large fists, but Malcolm continued to cower beneath him. I wanted to say that Malcolm was acting, but frankly it looked to me like Malcolm was truly afraid of Iron Horn. Not that I blamed him; Iron Horn looked like he was chiseled out of marble.

But the two G-Men were clearly distracted, so I pulled back again, crawled a little ways away from the roof, and then pressed the button on my suit-up watch. My suit shot out and in a second I was suited up again and ready to fly.

Standing up, I looked up at the sky, preparing to take off, when, without warning, a voice behind me said, "Where do you think *you're* going?"

I looked over my shoulder and saw a woman standing inside the door in the roof that led to the school's interior. She had extremely pale skin and very dark hair. She didn't look much older than me—maybe in her late teens or early twenties—but her short hairstyle looked really old-fashioned.

But what really stood out to me was her clothes. She wore a G-Men uniform, complete with the patch on her right shoulder. That meant that she was a G-Man, but I didn't recognize her at all, though that wasn't saying much, because I didn't know who most of the G-Men were.

"Who are you?" I said, turning to face her. "And where did you come from? I thought the government only sent two agents to protect he school."

"Call me Shade," said the woman. "I'm a new agent, having just signed up two months ago. As for what I'm doing here, did you really think that the government would only send *two* agents to protect a school from Master Chaos himself? Black Gold and Iron Horn are strong, but they couldn't beat Chaos by themselves."

I stepped backwards. I intended to just fly away and leave this woman behind, but something about her voice made it hard for me to ignore her. I noticed that her shoes seemed to blend in with the shadows, which looked weird, almost like she didn't have feet at all.

"Shade, huh?" I said. I immediately touched my face. "Did you see me suit-up?"

"Sadly, no," said Shade, shaking her head. "I was doing my rounds and came up here just when you put your suit on. That was your work, I presume?"

"Yes," I said. "I don't know if you recognize me, but I'm Bolt."

"I know all about you," said Shade. "I did my research on Silvers before I was assigned to this place. You're the new kid in town, aren't you?"

I didn't like an established superhero calling me the 'new kid,' because it reminded me too much of Robert, so I said, "Yeah. What about you? What kind of powers do you have?"

Shade chuckled. "Do you really think I'm just going to tell you? You really must be new, because you don't just reveal your powers to whoever asks, especially if they're a stranger or enemy."

"Uh huh," I said. "Let me guess based on your code name, then. You can control shadow, right?"

"Good guess," said Shade, which I noticed wasn't an affirmation or a denial. "But I have other powers, too, though I'll let you find out about them yourself rather than tell you. It's a lot more fun that way."

The way she used the word 'fun' made me uncomfortable, so I said, "Listen, Shade, I don't want to waste time talking with you. I'm trying to leave the school and stop Master Chaos, so if you would just let me leave, that would be great."

"Sorry, but I can't 'just let you leave,'" said Shade, shaking her head. "Director Smith gave us orders to make sure that *no one* leaves the school without our knowledge. And Director Smith isn't very tolerant of agents who don't follow orders, so I'm going to have to stop you."

I sighed. "I don't want to fight you. I don't really know what your powers are, but I doubt you have super strength. If I hit you, I'll probably end up hurting you or even killing you. Trust me, lady, we'd both be better off if we didn't fight."

"I don't need super strength to hold you down," said Shade. She smirked. "Look at your feet."

I looked down at my feet and was surprised to see that they were covered in shadow. I tried lifting my right foot up, but the shadow was like really sticky glue; I couldn't raise my foot even one inch.

I looked up at Shade again, who was still smirking. "What's going on? Why can't I move?"

"It's one of my powers," said Shade. "You guessed correctly that I can control shadow. What you didn't guess, however, is that I can use my shadow to hold down anyone I want. You can't use your super strength to break it, either, because unlike, say, chains or rope, shadow can't be snapped or broken."

I tried to prove her wrong by accessing my super strength and yanking my feet out of the shadows, but the shadow was as stubborn as a rock. I struggled, but the shadow didn't even budge.

"You really shouldn't strain yourself," said Shade, causing me to look up at her. "Just take it easy while I go get Black Gold and Iron Horn. They'll be so jealous when they see that I didn't let myself get distracted by some silly kid."

"You have to let me go," I said. I gestured at the sky. "I have to stop Master Chaos. I'm the only one who can."

"And you have a messiah complex, too," Shade observed. "I'm not sure if that is a super power or not, though, since most neoheroes tend to have it."

"It's not a messiah complex," I said. "Master Chaos is after me, so I'm going to meet him on my own terms. It's the only way to keep my friends and family safe."

"Oh, right," said Shade. "I heard Master Chaos tried to kill you with one of the military weapons he stole. But really, defeating Master Chaos isn't your responsibility. You should leave that to the adults."

I shook my head. "No. It's my duty to stop him."

"Why?" said Shade. "It's not like you let him out of Ultimate Max or anything. I'll let you go back to lunch if you promise not to run away and try to track down Master Chaos on your own."

I gritted my teeth. I wasn't going to reveal my secret identity to this woman now. But I still needed to escape. How?

Super strength didn't work, and I had a feeling that flight wouldn't do anything for me, either. That left me with no options, no options except for one: Super speed, perhaps the only power I hadn't actually mastered or even practiced yet. I wanted to, but Dad had insisted on using super strength and flight first.

The problem was that I didn't really know how to use my super speed due to my lack of training. I figured it probably worked the same way as my other powers, so I closed my eyes and started imagining myself running as fast as possible. It was pretty easy to do, because I had already seen online videos of other neoheroes who could run fast, but I didn't know if accessing my own super speed would be as easy as learning how to fly or using my super strength was.

Then I felt something in my legs. I opened my eyes and looked at my legs, which were starting to move, but were not yet free of this shadow. Still, I could tell that if I just kept it up, I might free myself.

I looked up at Shade, expecting her to notice me trying to escape, but instead she seemed focused on her communicator. It sounded like she was telling Black Gold and Iron Horn to get here, which made me want to leave even faster.

I tugged at the shadow holding me down. I wish I understood how it even worked, but I guess it didn't matter. I could feel my legs getting stronger and faster. Although the shadow was still thick and heavy, I could feel it becoming lighter and I knew I could escape as long as I kept it up.

"You've gone awfully quiet," said Shade suddenly, causing me to look at her again. "Don't have anything else to say to me?"

I shook my head. "Nope. Because I'm going to be getting out of here pretty soon and don't want to waste any time talking with you."

"How do you plan to do that?" said Shade, folding her arms over her chest. "Are you going to convince me to let you go?"

Again, I shook my head. I glanced at my legs, which were getting faster and faster as I pulled more and more at the shadow clinging to my feet. "Nah. I'm just going to free myself."

"Impossible," said Shade. "No one can escape my shadow without my permission or without light powers. Besides, Black Gold and Iron Horn should be here soon, so you don't have the time to escape."

"Tell yourself that all you like, lady, but it isn't going to help," I said. My legs were now moving up and down so rapidly that I could barely even see them.

Shade finally seemed to notice my rapidly moving legs, because her eyes focused on them for a second before she looked back up at my face. "What are you doing? Using your super strength?"

I grinned. I could actually feel the shadow starting to become less clingy, which meant that any second now I would be free. "Well, I'm just taking your advice: Never reveal your powers to a stranger or an enemy. And right now, I'd say you count as both."

Shade stepped forward, but she was too late. I immediately jumped upwards, using my super speed to give me an extra boost. The shadow clung to my legs like slime, but I activated my flight powers and shot into the sky as fast as I could. The shadow actually snapped around my feet, sending me hurtling into the sky almost faster than I could control myself.

Nonetheless, I regained control of my trajectory and flew as far and fast from the school as I possibly could. I glanced over my shoulder to see Black Gold and Iron Horn burst onto the school roof. Like Shade, they were staring up at me in surprise, but they were too far away to catch me now.

And I wasn't going to let them. I increased my speed and flew as fast and hard as I could, not caring what direction I was going in. I just wanted to get as far away from John Smith High School as I could. Once I was safely out of their range, I would figure out where to go from there.

CHAPTER EIGHTEEN

I FLEW HIGH INTO the sky, well above the clouds, until soon the earth was no longer visible to me. Even so, I didn't let up on my speed just yet. I kept expecting the G-Men to follow me, even though I knew that none of the G-Men in charge of protecting the school could fly. If any of them could, they would have come after me already.

But flying wasn't as easy as it seemed, so eventually I slowed down to a much more reasonable speed. I looked over my shoulder again, just to be sure that no one was following, and once I saw that I was alone, I started thinking about where I should go now.

My mission hadn't changed: Find Master Chaos and stop him for good before he could harm anyone I cared about. The only problem, of course, was that I didn't know where Master Chaos was. Texas, after all, was a big state. He could be in the Panhandle, in the hill country, at the Gulf, or anywhere else. And I didn't even know Texas all that well, having just moved down here a few weeks ago. I could probably spend days or weeks flying all over the state looking for him. That would just increase the chance that I would be caught by the G-Men or even by Dad, who I knew would probably start searching for me the second he learned of my little escape.

I stopped in midair, thinking about where I needed to go. Assuming Master Chaos was already in Texas—which I considered a safe assumption, because I doubted that his transforming robot would have been able to fly from New York to Texas without being noticed—then Master Chaos was probably already somewhere near Silvers. He could be hiding in the countryside, which would make sense, seeing as there were fewer people out there, but at the same time, that seemed too logical. I bet the G-Men and NHA were already scouring the countryside for him, which would make it a bad place to hide. Besides, Chaos still needed food and other necessities, which are kind of hard to get if you don't make it yourself or live near a town or city that you can buy it from. And if he was in Texas, then he probably also wanted to be near his family.

That was when I realized the most likely location of Master Chaos: Fallsville, where the Fallsville General Hospital—and his son, Robert Candle—was located.

-

Figuring out what direction Fallsville lay in was a difficult task, mostly because my sense of direction in the sky was shot. I had to look up the directions to the city on my suit-up watch, which showed me that it was about a hundred miles north. That might have sounded far away, but when you can fly as fast as a jet, it usually isn't much longer than a car trip to the supermarket.

Within minutes, the city of Fallsville came into view below. It wasn't exactly a huge city, but it was much bigger than Silvers. I saw lots of cars below on the highways and roads around and in the city, but I stayed as high in the sky as I could so I would not be noticed.

THE SUPERHERO'S TEST

The question now was, where should I go? Fallsville may not have been a huge city, but it would still take a long time to search, especially for a villain as crafty and deceptive as Master Chaos. Besides, I wasn't as familiar with Fallsville as I was with Silvers, so I would probably just end up getting lost.

Then I remembered that Robert was still in the Fallsville General Hospital. I considered whether or not I should go and talk with him, because he might know where his father was. Would Robert actually tell me where his father was, though? I doubted it. Robert obviously respected and cared about his father a lot. There was no way he'd tell me, even if he knew where his father was.

But maybe I could get some clues from him anyway. Or maybe I would find some clues in his hospital room that would help me locate Master Chaos. It was the only option I had at this point, so I flew over to the hospital, which was easy to find, because it was one of the largest buildings in the city.

Landing in the back of the hospital, I hid behind the dumpster and sent my suit back into my suit-up watch. Then I peered out from behind the dumpster, searching for anyone who might be nearby, but like on my last trip, the area behind the hospital was empty.

Sighing in relief, I walked around the hospital to the entrance. I could have tried breaking in again, but without Dad's gear to make that easy, I couldn't risk it. This was a job for Kevin Jason, not Bolt, although I was ready to put my suit on again if necessary.

The lady at the front desk was friendly and told me where Robert's room was after I explained to her that I was a friend from school who wanted to visit him. That was a lie, obviously, but the lady didn't know that, nor did anyone else in the hospital, either. I noticed a hospital security camera in the corner of the lobby, but I didn't think much of it, because I doubted that the security guards watching the camera would know who I was or why I was here.

Soon I entered Robert's room and found myself standing behind the floral curtains between the door and the rest of the room. Then I stopped and listened. I expected Robert to ask me who I was, but I heard nothing, which made me think that Robert might have perhaps gone to use the bathroom or maybe had even been checked out of the hospital already.

Then I heard loud snoring. Pushing aside the curtains between the door and the rest of the room, I saw Robert lying on his bed. He wasn't in his full-body cast anymore, but his arms and legs were still in casts and he looked like he had a long way to go before he was going to recover. His right hand was stuffed into his shirt, probably to keep it warm or something.

Aside from Robert, the room was empty. I walked as silently as I could, looking around the room for anything that might help me find Master Chaos, like a gift with an address on it or something. But the room looked the same as it had the last time I was here, which meant that this trip may have been pointless. But I didn't give up. I walked over to the drawers under the TV and started quietly pulling them open and searching their contents for anything that might help me find Master Chaos's location.

But just as I opened the first drawer, I heard Robert groan behind me, causing me to freeze. I looked over my shoulder and saw that Robert was waking up. He was yawning and his eyes were starting to flicker open, though he didn't seem to be entirely awake just yet.

THE SUPERHERO'S TEST

My first instinct was to run out the door like a mad man and never look back, but I caught myself. I knew Robert wouldn't be happy to see me, but maybe if I was polite, I could get him to talk with me and we could have a civilized discussion. I mean, he certainly couldn't punch me in the face, after all, what with his arms being broken and everything, which might help civilize him a little.

So, as casually as I could, I walked up to Robert, who was now shaking his head. He didn't seem to recognize me yet, but that was okay, because I figured that once he did, he'd want to tear me limb from limb.

"Hey, Robert," I said, stopping by his side, a polite smile on my face. "How are you doing? Feeling better?"

Robert looked at me. At first, there was no recognition in his eyes, but the more he looked at me, the more recognition I saw in his eyes. I half-expected him to start shouting obscenities at me or maybe call for the hospital staff to escort me out of the room.

But then Robert said, in a very weak voice, "Kevin? Is that you?"

I was surprised. That was the first time Robert had actually used my name, rather than calling me 'new kid.' That made me worried, but maybe Robert was in some kind of medically-induced personality change. I didn't know what they were pumping into him to help him deal with the pain, after all, though I still kept my distance just to be safe.

"Yes, it's me," I said. "I came to visit you in the hospital."

"Why?" said Robert. His voice was bitter. "So you could mock me or maybe punch me through another wall?"

"No, of course not," I said, shaking my head. "I'm sorry for doing that, Robert. I didn't mean to hurt you. I didn't even know that I could. I'm here for a different reason."

"What is that?" said Robert. He still sounded bitter, but also a little curious.

"I want to stop your dad, Master Chaos," I said. "And I think you're the only one who can tell me where he is."

Robert looked away from me, a scowl on his face. "Why should I help you? And why would I know where my dad is? I haven't spoken with him since he went to prison. Or ever, actually."

"Because I know you've been in contact with your dad," I said.

Robert looked at me in alarm. "What? How did you—"

"Shh," I said, holding a finger up to my lips. "It doesn't matter how I know. I just do. Otherwise I wouldn't be here."

Robert's alarm was replaced by annoyance. He held up a remote in his hand, his thumb hovering over one of the buttons. "Tell me, why shouldn't I call the hospital staff and tell them that you're harassing me and making my recovery difficult? I can do that, you know, even if I can't throw you out of my room myself."

"Because your dad isn't as good as you think he is," I said. "I don't know what stories your mom has been telling you about him, but your dad is a psycho who needs to be stopped before he hurts innocent people. And I'm the only one who can do that."

"But Father said that he wants to avenge me," said Robert. His eyes narrowed. "He knows what you did to me. He's going to kill you, like you deserve."

"Maybe he will, but do you think he'll stop with me?" I said. "I don't know what Master Chaos's plans for the future are, but I bet he's planning to hurt way more people than just me."

"Who cares?" said Robert with a shrug, but then he winced, likely because the shrug caused him pain. "Father will protect me and Mother. As long as he does that, I don't care if he kills everyone else on the planet."

"Come on, Robert," I said. "Your dad isn't the hero you think he is. He's a madman who wants to cause lots of destruction and chaos. He probably doesn't even care if you or your mom get hurt in the process."

Robert glared at me with such hatred that I actually stepped back. "Don't you dare say that about Father. He broke out of prison just for me. He would never hurt me or Mother. Never."

"Can you be so sure about that?" I said.

"Yes, I can," said Robert. He coughed. "Why wouldn't I be?"

"Well, think about it," I said. "Your dad only broke out of prison *after* you were nearly killed. If he was such a great dad, why didn't he break out earlier so he could be with you and your mom? Wouldn't you have benefited from having your dad in your life?"

Robert just scowled even more, but I could tell that I had got him. He didn't have a response for that, probably because I had touched a nerve. I didn't know what it was like being raised by a single parent, but I had some friends back in New York who were raised by their mothers and they always missed their fathers. I figured Robert was probably the same.

I noticed that Robert's thumb was on the button on the remote that would probably summon the hospital staff. I expected him to press it any second now, which would mean that I'd have to leave and resume my search for Master Chaos elsewhere.

But then Robert took his thumb off the remote and sighed. "Okay, Kevin, you made a good point. I don't know where Father is, but Mother gave me a few clues about where he is. I can tell you them if you want."

I nodded eagerly. "Great. I'm all ears."

"But you have to come closer," said Robert. He coughed again. "My voice is getting weak, so I want you close enough to hear without me having to raise my voice."

I drew closer to Robert's bed until I was standing right up against it. I leaned close to Robert's face, turning my ear to his mouth to make sure I didn't miss anything.

"All right," I said. "What are the clues to your dad's location?"

At first, Robert looked like he was too tired to speak. But then he pulled something out of his shirt and slammed it into my chest with surprising force.

Though the impact didn't hurt, I was nonetheless sent stumbling backwards. I looked down at my chest to see a strange, blinking star-shaped device attached to my chest.

Alarmed, I looked up at Robert, who was now smirking at me with triumph.

"Is this a bomb?" I said. I tried to remove it, but the thing would not come off. "Are you going to blow us both to pieces?"

Robert shook his head. "No. You're just going to meet Father, like you always wanted. Say hi to him for me."

I didn't understand what that meant until the star-shaped device on my chest glowed with a great white light, completely obscuring my view of Robert.

In the next second, the light vanished and I found myself standing alone in a dark room that clearly wasn't Robert's hospital room.

"What?" I said. I looked around, but could not see anything. "What happened? Where am I?"

Then the lights turned on. The sudden brightness briefly blinded me, but my eyes adjusted rapidly until I could now see someone standing in front of me.

And that someone was Master Chaos himself.

CHAPTER NINETEEN

MASTER CHAOS LOOKED A little different from the pictures I'd seen of him on the Internet. For one, he was in an old orange jumpsuit that had splashes of red, blue, and green paint on it. He was almost bald, too, with only a few wisps of hair peaking out from under his cowboy hat. He was much taller and bulkier than me, wearing thick rubber boots that were completely mismatched. He smelled weird, too, like sewage, as if he hadn't taken a shower in his life.

But his eyes … those were just as crazy as the eyes I had seen in the photos. They were extremely bloodshot, looking almost red, like he hadn't gotten any sleep for months.

I didn't know what to do. I hadn't expected to meet him so soon. I just stood there, staring at him, unable to look away from his mad eyes.

Then Master Chaos pushed up the brim of his hat and said, "Disappointing."

His voice was harsh and hoarse, very different from Robert's voice and not what I was expecting to hear.

That was why it snapped me out of my shock and caused me to say, "What?"

"You," said Master Chaos. He shook his head. "So small and scrawny. I thought that was just how the pictures made you look.

But I guess the camera must add ten pounds or something."

Master Chaos seemed very laid-back, like we were a couple of Internet friends meeting in real life for the first time. I almost wondered if he had forgotten the whole reason I was even here, but I didn't let my guard down around him.

"How did I get here?" I said. I touched the device on my chest. "How did Robert get this device?"

"Robby?" said Master Chaos. He seemed to notice the star-shaped device on my chest. "Ah, yes. I remember. I gave that to Maria, who then smuggled it into the hospital to give to him. It can teleport a person to a pre-programmed location. I didn't expect him to actually use it so soon, though, but hey, I'm not complaining."

"You mean you made this?" I said, glancing down at the device that was still stuck securely to my chest. "How?"

"I'm a genius," said Master Chaos, tapping the side of his face. Then he suddenly scowled, looking very much like his son. "Well, not *that* Genius, who I intend to butcher like a pig the next time I see him, but I'm still brilliant. Mad, yes, but brilliant."

"So you actually made this on your own?" I said.

"Oh, actually, I didn't really make it myself," said Master Chaos. "See, I stole some weapons from the government recently and the prototype for that device was among them. I tinkered with it a little and made it more appropriate for my purposes."

I tried to remove it from my chest, but it still wouldn't come unstuck. "So you gave it to Robert to teleport me here?"

"Of course," said Master Chaos. "I believed that you would come to visit Robby at some point, maybe to ask for forgiveness or mock him. I wanted Robert to have this so he could teleport you directly to me so I could punish you properly."

I looked up at Master Chaos again, whose smile revealed a row of crooked, blackened teeth. He really didn't seem to understand the concept of dental hygiene, or hygiene in general, based on how bad he smelled.

"So you never intended to attack me at my house at all," I said.

"Of course not," said Master Chaos. "Your house is too well-protected. The NHA and the G-Men expected me to do that. Because I am the personification of chaos, I can't very well do what they *expect* me to do, now can I?"

I looked around the area in which we stood. It looked like the interior of an old, abandoned warehouse, with sealed crates full of who-knows-what stacked all around us. The lights on the ceiling were weak, though the light streaming in from outside made it less dark than it would have been.

I had no idea where I was, but it didn't matter. I looked at Master Chaos again and said, "Well, this is exactly where I wanted to be. Say hello to my fist, Chaos!"

I ran at him, pulling back one of my fists. Master Chaos didn't move. He didn't even look alarmed. He just stood there, smiling, like he was amused. Well, he wasn't going to be amused when I punched my fist straight through his body and tore out his stomach.

With a yell, I punched Master Chaos directly in the stomach as hard as I could. But, even though my fist connected, Master Chaos didn't even flinch.

Instead, pain shot up my arm. It was like I had punched a brick wall. I yelled in pain and grabbed my fist, which felt broken into pieces. As a result, I didn't notice Master Chaos's own fist coming at me until it was too late.

Master Chaos's fist struck me in the abdomen, causing me to go down hard. I fell onto the floor and lay there, stunned, the breathe knocked out of me. I blinked several times before looking up at Master Chaos, who bent over, grabbed me by the neck, and lifted me off my feet.

I struggled to break his grip on me, but Master Chaos's grip was too strong. I tried punching and kicking his arm, but it was like I didn't even have any superpowers at all. He tightened his grip around my throat, causing me to gasp and stop punching and kicking at him.

"Why ... can't ... I ... hurt you?" I said, barely able to speak.

"The device on your chest," said Master Chaos, nodding at my chest. "Not only can it teleport you to me, but it can also negate your powers for an hour. Very useful when dealing with stupid kids like you."

"Negates my powers?" I said. "How?"

"I don't know," said Master Chaos with a shrug. "The government has apparently been trying to figure out how to de-power superhumans for a while. This isn't the only weapon I stole from them that can negate superpowers, but it is the only one I'll need to kill you."

"Are you going to kill me here and now, then?" I said.

"No," said Master Chaos, shaking his head. "Granted, it would satisfy my desire for revenge to do that, but you see, it wouldn't be very fun or dramatic. Let me show you how you will die."

Master Chaos carried me over to the center of the warehouse.

His grip loosened around my neck slightly, probably so I wouldn't fall unconscious on the way there, but his grip was still impossibly tight and there was no way I could break free from it. So I let him carry me around like a doll, knowing that each moment could easily be my last.

In the center of the warehouse was a strange set-up that looked like it came straight from a bad comic book. There was a large metal sheet with thick steel clamps for my arms and legs, while next to it was a vat of some kind of bubbling acid that looked like it could eat through titanium. Opposite the vat and metal sheet was a camera that appeared to be off, which stood next to a table that had a laptop on it, and sitting behind the laptop was a middle-aged Hispanic woman: Maria Candle, Master Chaos's wife and Robert's mother. She was typing away on the laptop, though I didn't know what she was typing.

"Oh, honey," said Master Chaos as he walked over to the metal sheet and the acid vat. His tone became sickeningly sweet. "Look what I found."

Maria looked up at us and actually smiled, though it was not a very comforting smile in my opinion. She stood up and walked around the table to us, moving very fast like she did not want to waste even one second.

"How wonderful!" said Maria, putting her hands together as she drew closer to us. "I didn't know we'd catch him so soon. I thought for sure that it would be another week or two before we got him."

"Well, honey, you clearly underestimated my genius," said Master Chaos. He leaned over and kissed her briefly, which was the most disgusting thing I'd seen in my life. "But I really couldn't have done it without you. Or Robert. I am the luckiest man in the world and couldn't ask for a better, more supportive family."

"You should take more credit for your success, Bernie," said Maria, her tone every bit as sickeningly sweet as Master Chaos's, if not more so. "After all, you were the one who devised this brilliant plan to avenge our son. I couldn't have come up with it on my own."

If Master Chaos hadn't already been choking me, I would have been gagging. I would never have thought of Master Chaos as a family man. I mean, I knew that Maria and Robert loved him, but it was hard for me to imagine one of the most vicious supervillains in the world being a family man. It felt like I had walked into some kind of alternate universe, even though I knew I hadn't.

"Well, you know what they say," said Master Chaos, "behind every great man is a woman. And you, Maria, are that woman, both to me and to Robert."

Please, God, just take me away from this mortal coil. Mom and Dad would understand.

"Anyway," said Master Chaos, his tone serious again. He looked at me and gestured at the acid vat with his free hand. "See that vat, Kevin? It is full of acid. And not the kind that makes you high, but the kind that will eat you alive. It's quite painful. I should know; the stray cat I dipped into it made some funny sounds."

"So that's what you're going to do to me?" I said. I glanced at the metal sheet. "Lower me into the acid slowly so my death will be painful and agonizing?"

"Slowly? Of course not," said Master Chaos, shaking his

head. "What a waste of time that would be! No, we're going to dunk you into it. Like I said, the device on your chest has a time limit and we are certainly not going to let it run out and give you an opportunity to escape. We're not stupid."

"What's the camera for, then?" I said, glancing at the large, unwieldy camera set on a tripod.

"We're going to livestream your death on the Internet, of course," said Master Chaos. He frowned and then looked at Maria. "Did I say that right?"

Maria nodded. "Yes, dear, that's the correct terminology."

"Good," said Master Chaos. He shook his head. "I am just not all that good with this modern technology. That's why I'm glad I married you, though, because you are."

Maria blushed, while I just wanted Master Chaos to dunk me into the vat and get it over with.

Nonetheless, I said, "Why are you going to livestream my death online? Why not just kill me right away?"

Instead of answering my question, Master Chaos brought me over to the metal sheet and slammed me down on it. The blow made me gasp in pain, but before I could do anything, Master Chaos was already tightening the clamps down on my arms and legs.

"You do have a point," said Master Chaos, without looking at me as he tightened the clamps around my wrists and ankles. "It would be easier to kill you, but I want the whole world to know that I am *back* and mean business." He finished tightening the clamps and then stood up, looking down at me with a scary grin on his face. "Maria tells me that lots of people use this thing called the Internet to watch videos and get their news, so I decided to use it to show everyone my triumphant return to the superhuman scene."

"How many people will be watching?" I said.

"Hundreds of thousands, maybe even millions," said Master Chaos. "Enough people who will share the video on their social media accounts and tell their friends in real life about it. By the end of the hour, the whole world will know that Master Chaos is still as dangerous as ever."

Master Chaos sounded positively giddy about it, while I said, "How did you get such a large audience already?"

"Maria is a skilled computer hacker," said Master Chaos, nodding at his wife, who was typing away behind her laptop again. "She's using her skills—along with a few government devices I stole—to make sure that the video of your death will play on every computer, tablet, and smartphone screen in the world."

"All this, just for me?" I said. "But I'm just a teenager."

Master Chaos wagged a finger at me. "No, no, no. You're not just a teenager. You nearly killed my one and only son. Not only that, but I also know who your father is."

My eyes widened. "You do?"

Master Chaos grinned. "Of course. Your father is Genius, that idiot who separated me from my family so many years ago now. Unfortunately, you don't seem to have inherited his intelligence."

"How did you figure that out?" I said. I struggled against the clamps, but the device on my chest must have still been active, because the clamps didn't even budge.

"When my robot attacked you and Genius while you were training last week," said Master Chaos. "You see, the robot was recording footage of its fight with you two and sending it to me to watch in real time. I realized that Bolt had to be you due to your similar powers and appearance and I deduced that Genius had to be your father, because why else would a retired superhero train a newbie if there wasn't some sort of relation between them?"

"Wow," I said. "Dad was right. You really are clever."

"Of course I am," said Master Chaos. "But don't worry. I'm not going to reveal your identity to the public. There's no need. All the world needs to know is that anyone who harms my family will suffer the same fate as you, no matter how insignificant they may be."

Then Master Chaos walked over to a lever in the floor and pulled it down.

Suddenly, the metal sheet I was clamped down to was jerked up into the air. I would have fallen to the floor if I hadn't been clamped so tightly to the sheet. The sheet slowly moved to the left until I was hanging directly over the bubbling vat of acid below. I could smell its acidic scent, which made my stomach upset, but I was too terrified to even throw up. I didn't know what it felt like to be eaten alive by acid, but I didn't want to find out.

Master Chaos walked away from the lever, looking very excited. "How does it feel? Are you comfortable? If you aren't, don't worry, because soon you won't feel anything at all."

"Let me down," I said. I tried to hide the fear in my voice, but it was impossible. "Please, I didn't mean to almost kill your son. It was an accident."

"Do I look like I care?" said Master Chaos with a snort. "You are the son of my worst enemy. When I heard that Robert was at death's door, it caused me so much pain and sorrow, pain and sorrow I hope that Genius will feel when he loses his own son."

Then Master Chaos looked at Maria. "Maria, is the camera ready to start filming?"

Maria nodded, her eyes fixed on the laptop screen. "Yes, dear. I will get it started as soon as you are ready."

Master Chaos stood in front of the camera, with the vat and I behind him. He spread his arms and said, "Maria, you know that I am *always* ready to be filmed. Let's get the show rolling!"

Maria nodded once again and typed on the laptop. "All right. We start filming … right … now!"

A green light started flashing above the camera's lens as spotlights flashed from the ceiling and focused on us. I looked around in surprise at the spotlights, while Master Chaos looked directly into the camera.

"Welcome, one and all, to the greatest show on the planet," said Master Chaos. He gestured behind himself. "I am Master Chaos, your host for this show. Today you will get to see a very special event: The death of Kevin Jason, the teenager who nearly killed my son. Why don't we start? I'm sure it will be fantastic."

CHAPTER TWENTY

I HAD ALWAYS DREAMED of being famous and having my own Internet show. In fact, when I was thirteen, I actually started my own YouTube channel, but I sort of abandoned it because no one watched my videos and all of the comments I got were really mean anyway.

But having my death livestreamed onto the Internet was not how I imagined making my debut as an Internet star. I struggled to break free of my clamps as hard as I could while Master Chaos continued speaking to the camera. He spoke really well, which made me wonder if he had been a public speaker before going into full-time villainy.

"Now, my viewers, you might be asking, 'Master Chaos, why are you killing a teenager? Why not kill someone like Omega Man or some other famous neohero? Or perhaps one of those corrupt politicians everyone keeps complaining about?'" said Master Chaos. Then he pointed at me, while still keeping his eyes on the camera. "The answer, of course, is that none of them would have quite the same impact as killing the kid who almost killed my kid. They would be fun, but not ... satisfying."

Master Chaos started walking over to the lever that controlled the metal sheet to which I was attached, with the camera following him. "You see, a little known fact about me is that I am a family man. It isn't anywhere on my Neo Ranks page, as I have been informed, but that's because it has always been my little secret. Today, however, everyone in the world will know that I am a proud father."

Master Chaos stopped right next to the lever and rested his hand on it, but he didn't pull it yet. It was only a matter of time before he did, however, so I struggled harder than ever, even though I knew it was pointless.

"Like most parents, I care about my son more than anything in the world, except for my loving and supportive wife," said Master Chaos, shooting a loving glance at Maria. He put a hand on his chest. "It broke my heart when I heard that my son, Robert Candle, was almost killed by this kid. So I broke out of prison to teach him—and the world—a lesson."

It was no use. I felt like a weak teenage boy, which is what I was, but with my powers I was always much stronger. I looked up at the chains holding my sheet and noticed that they looked old and rusty. They held because I was very still, but what if I tried swaying back and forth? Maybe if I got enough moment going, they would snap.

So I began swaying back and forth as fast as I could, which was difficult due to the weight of the metal sheet, as Master Chaos continued speaking.

"And what might that lesson be, you ask?" said Master Chaos. "That lesson is simple: Anyone who harms my family— regardless of whether you are a powerful politician or a weak peasant—will face immediate and harsh retribution. There are no lengths I will not go to protect those I hold dear."

I managed to get the metal sheet to sway a little, but only

little. I didn't have the momentum to sway it as much as I wanted and I had no time to gain that momentum, either.

"Now—while I love sending ominous warnings to my enemies as much as anyone—I think it is time to get to the part you've all been waiting for," said Master Chaos. He smiled again, a smile even crazier than his last one. "The death of Kevin Jason!"

I watched in horror as Master Chaos pulled the lever back, shouting, "Let the screaming commence!"

But nothing happened. I looked up at the rusty steel chains, expecting to see them disconnect from the sheet and drop me into the acid below. Yet the chains didn't even budge.

Then I looked down at Master Chaos, who was staring at the lever in disbelief. He pushed and pulled it again, but still nothing happened.

"What the hell?" said Master Chaos. He looked over at Maria, who looked just as shocked as him. "Maria, what is this? What happened to the lever?"

"I-I-I don't know," said Maria. She started clicking and typing on the laptop. "I mean, it was working just a few seconds ago. There's no way it could have malfunctioned like that so fast."

"Maria, if you don't figure this out right away—" Master Chaos said, in a threatening voice, before he was interrupted by another voice.

"Threatening your wife for something she had no hand in doing?" said a familiar voice nearby. "Looks like you haven't change a bit, Bernard."

I looked to the right, as did Master Chaos, Maria, and even the camera, to see Dad—in full Genius attire—standing on top of one of the nearby crates. His arms were folded over his chest, which actually made him look cool. I never thought that Dad could ever look cool, which I attributed to the gas from the acid messing with my brain's perception of reality.

"Genius?" Master Chaos said. "What the—? Are you the reason my show has been ruined?"

Dad nodded. "Of course. I disabled the lever before you could use it to kill that innocent teenage boy. It was very easy to do."

"How did you even know where to find me?" said Master Chaos. "I thought no one knew where I was."

"I tracked the boy's smartphone," said Dad. "Easy enough to do with my technology. When the boy disappeared from his school earlier, I knew that he had to be in your clutches." Then Dad pointed at Master Chaos. "Now, Master Chaos, I am going to put you back behind bars, where scum like you belong."

Master Chaos clinched his fists and then shouted, "Chaos bots! Get him!"

Without warning, two large robots that looked like the one I fought last week burst out of a couple of crates and flew toward Dad with rocket boosters. Dad, however, jumped down from the crate, narrowly avoiding the robots as they flew past him. He tried to run toward Master Chaos, but then the robots landed in front of him, cutting off his path.

"Kill him!" Master Chaos roared, pointing at the robots. "Kill him dead!"

I wasn't sure how Dad was going to beat the two robots. They were much bigger and stronger than him; Dad didn't even have super strength like me.

But then, without warning, Seeker One—one of Dad's drones

—smashed through the windows and into the warehouse. It immediately started shooting lasers at the robots, striking them in the heads and make their heads explode. The now-headless robots collapsed to the floor, allowing Dad to jump over them and continue running over to Master Chaos.

Master Chaos, however, waved his hands at the chains holding me above the acid vat. Without warning, the chains snapped and I started falling to the vat below, screaming my head off and knowing that my death was mere seconds away.

But then Seeker One flew by and shot out a cable that wrapped around the hook to which the sheet had been attached. I abruptly stopped falling just inches away from the surface of the acid vat and was slowly but surely carried away from the acid's surface. Seeker One carefully laid my sheet down on the ground and then used its lasers to shoot the clamps off my wrists and ankles.

Sitting up, I looked over at Master Chaos, who was now running away. I got up to follow him, but then Dad—who was chasing Master Chaos—stopped and, looking at me, shouted, "Flee, boy! Go find the police and get to safety. I will deal with Master Chaos."

I immediately understood that Dad was telling me not to help. I was going to say no and follow Master Chaos anyway, but then I remembered that the camera was still rolling and if I put on my suit now, I'd blow my secret identity to the whole world.

Reluctantly, I nodded and then ran away between two crates. I heard the sounds of Dad and Master Chaos fighting behind me, but it was impossible to tell who was winning and who was losing. Seeker One flew above me, probably to escort me to safety, but before I could get very far, someone stuck their leg out from behind a crate in my path, which I tripped over and fell face first onto the floor.

Dazed, I looked up to see Maria Candle standing over me. Only now, she held a gun in her hand, which she was pointing directly at my face.

"Bernard may have failed to kill you, but that doesn't mean that I will," said Maria, sounding just as mad as her husband. "This is for Robert."

Right before Maria could pull the trigger, Seeker One's cable flew out of nowhere and struck her in the face. The blow knocked her flat off her feet, causing her to drop the gun, which I slapped away out of her reach.

But it turned out that I didn't need to do that, because Maria looked like she had been struck unconscious by the blow. Rising to my feet, I was about to resume running when I heard an explosion behind me. I looked over my shoulder, but my view of the fight between Dad and Master Chaos was blocked by the crates.

"Come on, Kevin," came a voice from Seeker One, which I recognized as Valerie's voice. "You heard your father. We must get you to safety so Master Chaos doesn't kill you."

"But I want to help Dad," I said, looking up at Seeker One. "What if Dad can't beat Master Chaos on his own?"

"He will," said Valerie matter-of-factly. "Genius beat him once before, after all. There's no reason he can't beat him again."

"I know," I said, my hands balling into fists. "But still, I'm the one who caused Master Chaos to escape. I should be the one to stop him or at least help Dad stop him."

"Genius gave me instructions to ensure that you got to safety after we freed you from Master Chaos's clutches," said Valerie. "I can go against my programming, but I would rather not, because Genius expects me to follow his every order."

"But what if he gets killed?" I said. "You know that Dad isn't as young as he once was. Master Chaos is old, too, but he's a lot crazier and more violent than Dad. Plus, he has those government robots on his side. Dad needs backup."

"You are correct," said Valerie. "That is why I have sent messages to the police, the G-Men, and the NHA with the location of Master Chaos so they can get here to help your father."

"How long will it take for them to get here?" I said.

"It is different for each group, but the police of Fallsville will take at least ten minutes to drive here," said Valerie.

"Ten minutes?" I said. "Valerie, we don't *have* ten minutes. A lot can happen in ten minutes." I gestured at the device on my chest. "Look, this device Master Chaos stole from the government is inhibiting my powers. It will deactivate on its own after a while, but not as fast as I'd like. Can you remove it with your lasers so I can gain access to my powers again and help Dad?"

"I really shouldn't," said Valerie. "Genius already got angry at me once for helping you visit Robert Candle in the Fallsville General Hospital. I do not want to anger him again."

"I'll take the blame if he finds out," I insisted. "I'll tell Dad I forced you to do it. You don't need to worry about that."

Seeker One didn't really have a face, and as far as I knew, Valerie couldn't feel actual emotions, but I thought the drone looked somewhat sheepish. "Well ... okay. But this will be the

216

very last time I go against Genius's orders."

"Fine by me," I said. I gestured at the power inhibitor on my chest. "Get rid of it."

Seeker One shot a laser from its gun that struck the device, making it smoke and crackle. It also caused the device to loosen its grip on my chest, allowing me to rip it off and toss it onto the floor.

Then, without hesitation, I pressed the button on my suit-up watch and I was immediately covered in my suit. It felt good to be suited up again and to feel my super strength flowing through my veins.

I looked up at Seeker One and said, "Thanks! I'm going to help Dad now. You should go and wait for the police to arrive."

"Yes, sir," said Valerie. "Are you sure you won't need backup?"

I shook my head. "Dad and I have Master Chaos covered, so we'll be fine. You just make sure to let the police know what's going on."

"All right," said Valerie. "Be safe."

With that, Seeker One turned and flew away. I watched the drone fly away for a moment before turning around and flying toward the scene of the fight between Dad and Master Chaos, hoping to get there in time to help Dad.

CHAPTER TWENTY-ONE

LYING NEAR THE CEILING of the warehouse, I looked down and saw Dad and Master Chaos fighting near the acid vat, with the camera still filming their fight. Master Chaos was throwing punch after punch at Dad, but Dad—moving faster than I thought he could—kept dodging the punches and using his gauntlets to zap Master Chaos, although the electric jolts hardly seemed to faze Chaos.

It looked like they were evenly matched, so I was about to help Dad when I heard rocket boosters nearby and looked to the left to see yet another one of Master Chaos's 'Chaos bots,' as he called them, flying at me.

I dropped to the floor, narrowly avoiding the robot, which turned in the air and landed right in front of me, blocking my way to the fight between Dad and Master Chaos. The robot rose to its full height, easily three times as tall as me, and aimed its guns at me.

But I wasn't going to let this these stop me from helping Dad. I zoomed around it, dodging its bullets that struck the floor, crates, and ceiling as the robot vainly tried to shoot me. I jumped over the robot and then kicked out its knees from behind it, causing it to fall on top of me.

But I caught the robot as it fell onto me and tossed it into the acid vat. The robot sank into the acid, trying but failing to escape as the acid ate through its thick metal plating and its interior wiring. Electricity sparked and crackled as the acid destroyed it, but I didn't stop to watch it get destroyed. I ran around the vat, to the scene of the fight between Dad and Master Chaos.

Master Chaos was still trying to punch Dad, while Dad was still jolting him with electricity. But Master Chaos was too focused on Dad to notice me, so I ran and then jumped through the air, aiming to kick him in the head.

Then, at the last moment, Master Chaos grabbed me by the leg and threw me into Dad. We both flew across the floor and slammed into one of the crates, the impact sending splinters and chunks of wood flying everywhere, as well as sending out a huge pile of what looked like salt.

Shaking my head, I stood up and looked down at Dad, who wasn't moving.

"Dad?" I said, worry in my voice. I shook him, but Dad didn't move. "Dad? Dad!"

Suddenly, Dad groaned in pain and shook his head. He looked up at me, his expression hidden behind his helmet, but I could guess what he was thinking. "Bolt? What the hell are you doing here?"

I cringed at Dad's annoyance, but I said, "I want to help you defeat Master Chaos."

Dad groaned again and sat up. His armor was cracked by the impact, but he otherwise seemed okay. "You should leave. Master Chaos is a dangerous enemy, worse than his robots."

"No way," I said, shaking my head. "I came looking for Master Chaos because I wanted to stop him myself. I'm not going to run away now just because you think I can't defend myself."

Dad stood up, rubbing his back. He sighed. "Fine. I can see that you will not listen to your elder, as usual."

"What's that supposed to mean?" I said in annoyance.

Before Dad could respond, Master Chaos laughed, causing me to look over at him. He hadn't moved from his position, but he was now grinning like he had just heard a great joke.

"How touching," said Master Chaos with a sniffle. "Father and son teaming up to defeat me. It makes me wish that my own son was here to team up with me. This would be a great father-son bonding moment, you know."

"Your days are numbered, Master Chaos," I said, punching my hand into my fists. "Your days are numbered, whether you like it or not."

Master Chaos chuckled. "Many neoheroes have told me that. Very few have ever had the power to actually carry out that threat."

"Then count us among that few," said Dad, standing beside me. "I beat you once, Bernard. I can do it again."

"Oh, really?" said Master Chaos. "I've had sixteen years to stew over my last defeat to you, Genius. I'm not the same man that went into Ultimate Max. Behold!"

Master Chaos slammed his hands together. I immediately felt some kind of power wave blow out of his body, but didn't know what it was until all hell broke loose.

The lights in the ceiling suddenly exploded, raining down glass and wiring on us. The windows shattered, the crates blew up, and huge cracks appeared in the floor, which suddenly became tilted. I staggered to the side, while Dad was just barely keeping his balance.

"What's going on?" I said.

"Master Chaos's chaos power," said Dad, raising his arms to protect himself from the falling glass from the exploded lights above. "Watch out!"

I looked over to see Master Chaos coming at me. He seemed completely unaffected by the chaos happening around him. I tried to get a footing, but the cracked, tilted floor made that almost impossible.

As a result, Master Chaos managed to punch me in the face. The blow knocked me flat off my feet, but I managed to roll out of the way of his foot, which stomped the spot in the floor where I'd fallen.

Rising to my feet, I threw a punch at Master Chaos, who caught my fist and twisted my arm, making me cry out in pain. Then Master Chaos punched me again, this time with enough force to send me flying.

I crashed into a crate, the impact dazing me. Shaking my head, I looked at the interior of the crate and realized that I had crashed into a crate full of towels, which had absorbed some of the impact. Still, my head was spinning, so I rubbed it as I looked over at where Dad and Master Chaos were now fighting.

Despite having been smashed into a crate, Dad wasn't slowing down. He kept outside of Master Chaos's reach, ducking and dodging each blow. One of Master Chaos's blows went far off mark, leaving him defenseless. Dad raised his gauntlets, which began to glow with energy, but Master Chaos must have been bluffing with his last attack, because he immediately grabbed Dad's wrists and jerked his arms upwards.

Powerful lasers shot out of Dad's gauntlets and struck the ceiling, sending debris falling down on him and Chaos as they struggled against each other. Or rather, Dad struggled against Master Chaos, because Chaos held him in one spot and would not let him move.

Then Master Chaos tightened his grip around Dad's gauntlets, causing them to crack and spark. Dad groaned in pain, but there was nothing he could do to stop Chaos, who was far more powerful than him.

"Dad!" I shouted.

I shot out from the crate and body-slammed Master Chaos, sending him flying. He crashed into some crates nearby, but I didn't pay attention to that. Dad fell onto his knees, holding his crushed gauntlets out, still groaning in pain.

"Dad, are you okay?" I said, kneeling beside him to look at his wrists. "Your arms—"

"Broken," said Dad. He groaned again. "Arms and gauntlets."

"Then we need to get you medical attention," I said. "I can fly you out of here to—"

"No," said Dad, shaking his head. "Master Chaos needs to be stopped. If we leave now, he'll just get away."

I looked over in the direction I had punched Master Chaos, but it didn't look like he had recovered yet. Looking at Dad again, I said, "Don't you think your health's more important than beating Master Chaos?"

"No," said Dad. "But I don't think I'll be able to beat him. Can't use my tech without my hands."

I stood up. "Then I'll beat him into a bloody pulp. Won't take five minutes."

THE SUPERHERO'S TEST

"You can't beat him with sheer strength alone," said Dad. "The first time I beat him, I outwitted him. He'll pummel you to pieces, even with your super powers."

"Then how am I supposed to beat him?" I said.

"I don't know," said Dad. "But you won't be able to beat him."

I scowled. Master Chaos was going to get up again soon. Once he did, the fight would resume, but if Dad was right, it was a fight we were destined to lose. And, although I hated to admit it, I wasn't as clever as Dad, so I wouldn't be able to outwit Master Chaos, either.

But then an idea occurred to me. It was a crazy idea, but it had a good chance of working. I looked down at Dad and said, "Dad, does your belt still work?"

"Yes, it does," said Dad, nodding. "Why?"

"I need it," I said. "Just long enough to use it against Master Chaos."

I couldn't see Dad's expression due to the visor of his helmet, but he said, "Fine. Take it and use it for whatever you need."

I immediately removed Dad's utility belt and tied it around my waist just as I heard movement in the debris under which Master Chaos was buried. A second later, Master Chaos burst out of the debris. His eyes were even madder, his hat was missing, and his face was bloody, but he seemed more ready than ever to resume fighting.

"Well, that was a refreshing nap," said Master Chaos, his mad grin revealing that he was missing a few teeth now. He cracked his neck. "Now I'm ready to finish what I started."

I flew over and landed in front of him, putting myself between him and Dad. I folded my arms across my chest and met Master

Chaos's crazy eyes. "If you want to kill Dad, then you have to go through me first."

"Oh, you naïve brat," said Master Chaos, chuckling. "You are just like your father, defiant to the end. It will be a pleasure tearing your spine from your body."

Master Chaos immediately ran toward me. I raised my hands in time to catch his massive fists as they came flying at me. I skid backwards, doing my best to hold him back, but Master Chaos was ridiculously strong. He didn't even seem to be trying to push me, while I was doing everything I could to hold back.

But eventually, I found my footing and started pushing back. This time, I actually managed to keep Master Chaos from forcing me back and the two of us struggled against each other for several seconds, our strength briefly matched equally.

Then, without warning, Master Chaos slammed his foot into my stomach. The blow knocked the air out of me, causing me to lose my breath and my footing.

As a result, Master Chaos raised me above his head and slammed me onto the ground. I tried to get up, but then he smashed his boot into my face, the blow making my head spin.

"Now you stay down, silly boy," said Master Chaos, though his voice sounded strange due to how dizzy I was. "First, I will kill Genius. Then I will come back to finish you."

Master Chaos walked over me, seemingly convinced that I was down. And yeah, I did find it hard to think straight or focus again, because my head was throbbing. I felt blood leaking from my forehead and I was pretty certain that my ribs were broken, if not shattered completely.

Still, I forced myself to rise to my feet and turned to face

THE SUPERHERO'S TEST

Master Chaos, who was walking away from me. "Why don't you finish your fight with me first, instead of running away to fight my old man?"

Master Chaos sighed, stopped, and turned around to look at me. "What will it take for you to stay down? Regardless, I was going to kill you anyway. That's the whole reason I broke out of prison in the first place, after all."

Chaos stepped towards me, but I activated my super speed and zoomed behind him in a flash. Before Chaos could react, I removed Dad's utility belt from my waist, tied it around his, and then turned the Teleportation Buckle.

Master Chaos only had enough time to look down at the belt in surprise before he vanished into thin air. It was instantaneous. One moment he was there; the next, he was completely gone.

Panting, I wiped the blood off my brow and looked over at Dad. Dad was staring at me, probably with surprise, although again his helmet made it hard to tell.

"What … what happened?" said Dad.

"Teleported him," I said. "Not sure where, but he's gone."

"What if you teleported him away?" said Dad in annoyance. "Now he's gotten away, and with my belt, too. All because I trusted you to—"

Dad was interrupted when Master Chaos crashed through the ceiling above. The supervillain crashed into one of the crates, which, based on the *clang* it made, was probably full of heavy, not very soft metal objects.

"There he is," I said, pointing at the crate. I smirked at Dad. "What were you saying about me letting him get away?"

I could tell I got Dad that time, because he just said, in an annoyed voice, "Don't get too cocky. Go check on him and make sure he's down for good"

I nodded, still smirking, and flew over to the crate Master Chaos had crashed into. Landing on the edge of the crate, I peered inside and saw that Master Chaos had crashed into a bunch of heavy-looking hammers. Dad's utility belt was still tied securely around his waist, though Chaos looked like he had been knocked out completely. He had an especially ugly gash on the side of his head, making his face as red as a slab of uncooked beef.

Standing up, I looked over my shoulder at Dad and, giving him the thumbs up, said, "He's down! Now all we need to do—"

I heard the movement in the crate below too late. I looked down just in time for Master Chaos's massive hand to wrap around my throat and cut off my air supply. I gasped, but I couldn't speak.

Master Chaos was awake. His eyes were full of red anger; they were literally red, maybe because he got blood in them or something. He was breathing heavily and looked more like a beast now than a human.

"Good ... try," said Master Chaos. Every word sounded like it caused him great pain; his lungs must have been damaged or something. "Didn't see that coming. But I'm done treating you with kid gloves. Time to die."

His grip tightened so hard that I literally couldn't breathe. My vision kept blinking in and out. Even my super strength was starting to fail me. I panicked and tried to break free, but Master Chaos held me as tightly as a metal clamp.

This was it. I was dead. I was going to die and there was nothing I could do about it. I stopped trying to free myself and just accepted my death.

But then, through my oxygen-deprived brain, I heard Dad shout, "Self-destruct sequence activate!"

I had no idea what that meant until I heard a tiny beeping sound. Both Master Chaos and I looked down at the utility belt still attached to his waist. It was blinking red.

A second later, the belt exploded. The explosion tore me out of Master Chaos's grasp, sending me flying backwards through the air. I crashed onto the floor, rolling until I crashed into a crate. I immediately breathed in as much sweet air as I could, although it really wasn't as sweet as it could have been, mostly due to the dust in the air.

Still, eventually I breathed enough air back to help my senses return to normal. I looked up at the crate where Master Chaos had fallen, which now burned merrily and smelled like burning wood and melting metal. Aside from the crackling of flame, I heard nothing from Master Chaos.

Then I heard a groan behind me and looked over my shoulder to see Dad walking toward me. He was moving slowly—likely due to the fact that his wrists were broken—but he was walking nonetheless, the fire from the explosion reflected in his cracked visor.

"Dad?" I said. I coughed and sat up, rubbing the back of my aching head. "What was that?"

"The voice-activated self-destruct sequence I programmed into my belt in case it fell into the hands of anyone I didn't want having it," said Dad, stopping a few feet from me. He looked at the fiery mass of burning wood and metal. "It responds only to my voice. I wish I didn't have to use it, but your life is more important than my belt. I can make another belt, anyway."

I looked back at the burning crate and frowned. "Do you think Master Chaos—"

"Survived?" said Dad. "Unlikely. Master Chaos is powerful, but I designed the explosion to be powerful enough to kill neoheroes. He's probably little more than burnt meat now."

"So … he's gone?" I said. "We'll never have to fight him again?"

Dad nodded. "Yes."

I sighed in relief, but then heard another beeping. I thought it was yet another self-destruct sequence being activated, but then I looked over and saw that the beeping was coming from the camera that Maria Candle set up earlier. It was still active, still filming us, and surprisingly unscathed.

But just as I noticed that, I heard a loud *pop* and a chunk of burning wood shot out of the fiery crate and struck the camera, causing it to collapse. I looked at Dad, who had also noticed the camera.

"What do you think that means?" I said. "Do you think—"

"That millions of people around the world saw our fight and now know who you are?" said Dad dryly. "Yes. And I don't like that."

"Why?" I said curiously. "What's so bad about so many people watching our fight with Chaos?"

Dad shook his head. "I will explain later. For now, we need to get my arms looked at, which means we need to find your mother. And speak with the police, too, once they get here. Come on."

With that, Dad turned and started walking away from the crate. I scrambled to my feet and followed, feeling relieved that

THE SUPERHERO'S TEST

Master Chaos was gone, but also worrying about what was going to happen next. Because if Dad didn't like the fact that our fight with Master Chaos had been witnessed by tons of people all around the world, then I knew it was going to be a problem, even if I wasn't yet sure how.

CHAPTER TWENTY-TWO

HE NEXT WEEK WENT by like a blur to me, and it wasn't because of my super speed.

First, Dad and I spoke with the officers of the Fallsville City Police Department, who had arrived in front of the warehouse just as we were exiting it. Dad explained to them what happened, although briefly because we needed to get his arms medical attention quickly, and then told them that the NHA and the G-Men would arrive soon to clean up and recover Master Chaos's remains. He also told them that Maria Candle was still inside the warehouse and explained how she had helped Master Chaos. The police, surprisingly enough, actually listened to Dad's story and let us go, probably because Dad was such a famous superhero or maybe because he was working with the G-Men on the case.

Regardless, the officers let us go home. I suggested we fly, but Dad had Seeker One teleport us back with its prototype 'teleportation beam.' It worked similarly to the Teleportation Buckle, except you didn't have to wear it to use it. It felt weird to be teleported back home like that, but when I saw Mom's relieved face in the living room (which was where we reappeared), I forgot all about how weird it felt to teleport and was just happy that we had made it back home together.

When we got home, Dad had Mom work on his arms. Dad

said he didn't want to go to the hospital because he didn't want to risk people learning his secret identity. And Mom, apparently, had some experience fixing wounds inflicted from superhero battles, because she removed his gauntlets and went to work bandaging and splinting his arms like she had done it a million times.

While she did that, I told her what happened during our fight with Master Chaos. Mom listened, but didn't say much until the end when I mentioned that Master Chaos was dead. At that point, Mom almost burst into tears of joy, which made me try to calm her down because I was worried that her crying might distract her from helping Dad. I managed to get her to stop crying after a while, though I could tell she was still happy that we were safe. I also thought she was happy that we had avenged Uncle Jake, too, even if she didn't say it.

When Mom finished bandaging Dad's arms, I returned to my room. Mom said I still had school tomorrow and I was too exhausted to argue against that, so when I went to my room, I didn't even take off my super suit. I just fell onto my bed and slept through the entire day and into the morning in my suit. In fact, I was so tired that I almost was late for school, but Mom woke me up and I managed to use my super speed (very slightly, of course) to help me get to school on time.

When I got to school, I was immediately mobbed by the other students. I learned that everyone had seen me on Master Chaos's livestream and they wanted to know how that happened and how I got there. I frankly hadn't been able to come up with an explanation for that, but somehow I convinced them that Master Chaos had kidnapped me from within the school yesterday without anyone noticing. Of course, that made the three G-Men protecting the school look like idiots, but no one seemed to mind that. Everyone just seemed proud of the fact that they knew someone who had been almost murdered by one of the world's worst supervillains, which I guess was better than being treated with derision for being the new kid, at least.

At lunchtime, I learned from Malcolm that the Master Chaos livestream had been seen by millions of people all over the world and now the Bolt Neo Ranks page had hundreds of thousands of views from people trying to find out who I was. My Neo Rank had even gone up, from 1.5 all the way to 7, which was amazing, because very few neoheroes ever made that kind of leap on Neo Ranks. Even Tara seemed impressed by it, although she was more concerned with my health, asking if I was okay after being kidnapped by Master Chaos.

Not only that, but the three G-Men who had been tasked with protecting the school—Black Gold, Iron Horn, and Shade—were called back to Washington the day after. Dad told me that the police had confirmed that Master Chaos was indeed dead, which meant that there was no reason for the G-Men to protect my school anymore, although the police couldn't find Maria Candle and believed she had fled, though they did not know where. Frankly, I wasn't worried, because the G-Men put her on their most wanted list and offered a reward to anyone who could bring her in, so I figured they were going to capture her sooner or later.

Robert Candle's location, however, was perfectly well-known. He was back in school a couple of days later, except he had to rely on crutches to get around. I worried that Robert, who probably knew my secret identity, would tell everyone that I was Bolt, but he never did. That was probably because everyone thought Robert was crazy, a reputation he had gained after 'lying' about me punching him through the cafeteria wall. Still, every now and then Robert would shoot me a death glare, especially whenever anyone mentioned my alternate identity. The police, apparently, were not going to arrest him because they did not believe he had helped Master Chaos, which worried me a little, because Robert still held a grudge against me, and if he developed powers at some point, I had no doubt he'd use them against me somehow.

In any case, the rest of the week was the first time in a long time that I didn't feel stressed out or worried. I just went to school, hung out with Malcolm and Tara, and went home every day. I didn't even put on my super suit. As much as I enjoyed using my powers, my fight with Master Chaos had left me a little worn out with fighting evil for now. I still planned to resume superheroics someday—despite Mom and Dad's disapproval—but for now I decided I'd take things nice and easy and leave the superheroics to the NHA and the G-Men.

But then on Friday afternoon, as I returned home from school, I noticed a large black van in the driveway of our house. At first, I didn't think much of it, thinking that maybe Mom or Dad had invited one of the neighbors over or something, so when I entered the house, I shouted, "Mom! Dad! I'm home! Whose car is that out—"

I stopped speaking when I reached the living room, where I saw four people sitting.

Two of them were Mom and Dad. Mom wore her kitchen apron, looking like she had just been in the middle of cooking dinner (and I could smell spaghetti sauce from the kitchen), and was sitting in one of the recliners. Dad sat in the recliner next to her, his arms still in their splints. He had been sitting there for the last week, recovering from having his arms broken, so I didn't find that strange.

But what I did find strange were the two people sitting on the couch opposite my parents. One was a young woman in her twenties, with pale skin and dark hair and wearing a G-Men uniform. I recognized her as Shade, and she must have recognized me, too, because she smiled and waved at me when she saw me.

Sitting beside her was a man I'd never seen before. His hair was dark, like Shade's, but longer, with a few gray hairs scattered here and there. He also looked older than Shade, probably in his forties at least. He wore an old-fashioned suit, with a G-Men patch on his right shoulder, which meant he was yet another G-Man, though I didn't know which one.

When he looked at me, I felt like he was reading my mind. His eyes looked too old for his face, as old as my Grandpa's eyes, which was weird because this guy was obviously in his forties while Grandpa was in his nineties.

"Hello, Kevin," said the man. His voice was soft and gravelly. "Nice to meet you."

I stared at the man for a moment before looking at Mom and Dad. "Who are these people and why are they sitting on our couch?"

Dad sighed. He gestured with his fingers at the two. "Kevin, these two are from the G-Men. The young lady is Shade, who I have been told has already met you, and the second is—"

"Cadmus Smith," said the man, interrupting Dad. "Director of the Department of Superpowered and Extraterrestrial Beings and leader of the G-Men.''

Cadmus Smith spoke like he was reciting a line he had spent hours rehearsing. Based on the way Shade rolled her eyes, I could tell this wasn't the first time he had introduced himself that way.

"Wait, does that mean you're from the government?" I said, looking at Cadmus. "Why? Is it about Master Chaos? How long have you been here?"

"We arrived half an hour ago," said Cadmus. He leaned toward me, his gaze never breaking away from mine. "As for why we are here, yes, it is related to the Master Chaos incident, which we understand you were directly involved with."

I started and looked at Dad. "Dad, do they know—"

"That I'm Genius and you're Bolt?" said Dad. He nodded. "Yes."

"How?" I said. "I thought no one knew our secret identities."

Cadmus actually chuckled at that. "We in the G-Men have our ways of finding out the secrets of every person in the country when we need to. But don't worry. Due to your bravery, we will not publish your secret identities to the world."

I bit my lower lip, but Cadmus seemed to be telling the truth, so I said, "What are you doing here, exactly? Do you want to know more details about Master Chaos's death? Or maybe about Robert or Maria Candle?"

Cadmus shook his head. "No, no. Our forensic analysts already know everything there is to know about Master Chaos's death, probably even more than you do, and we have recovered every Project Neo weapon he stole from our facility, aside from a few whose location we are still searching for. And the Candles aren't our biggest priority at the moment."

"Then what is?" I said.

Cadmus pointed at me. "You are."

"No, he isn't," said Dad, before I could respond. "You know our answer."

Cadmus folded his hands over each other. "Theodore, I know what you said, but—"

"But what?" I said, looking between Dad and Cadmus in confusion. "What's going on?"

Cadmus looked at me again. "Allow me to explain: We are interested in offering you a position on the G-Men."

"Me?" I said, pointing at myself. "A G-Man? Why?"

"Because of your battle with Master Chaos," said Cadmus. "My superiors in the government were impressed with your bravery, skills, and ingenuity in dealing with one of the most dangerous supervillains in the country. With a little training, we believe you would make a great member of the G-Men."

I was too taken aback by this offer to say anything, but then Dad said, "Kevin is not joining the G-Men."

"Why not?" I said, looking at Dad in surprise. "Why can't I make this decision on my own?"

"Because you aren't old enough yet," said Dad. He glared at Cadmus and Shade. "And I trust the G-Men about as much as I trust the rest of our government, which is to say, very little."

Cadmus sighed and rubbed his temples. "Theodore, please, you know the G-Men have changed since the nineties. Kevin will be perfectly safe with us. We won't ask him to do anything morally questionable. We will only ask him to use his powers to serve his country."

"That's what you said last time," said Dad. His tone was

angry, angrier than I had heard him in a while, which surprised me. "And I remember well how your people tried to stab us in the back."

"Wait, what's going on?" I said. "What happened back in the nineties?"

Cadmus shrugged. "History, that's all. Something I had hoped that your father would have been able to forgive and forget, but apparently I was too optimistic."

"I'm not the only neohero—current or retired—who still hasn't forgiven you for that," said Dad. He nodded at the door. "Now get out. We don't want your kind here. And *do not* contact us again. Understand?"

For a moment, I thought Cadmus was going to say no and tell Shade to arrest Dad. I was willing to fight him if I had to, even though I didn't know if I could beat Shade in a fight, especially if she had help from Cadmus, whose powers I knew nothing about.

But then Cadmus nodded and said, "Very well. We will leave." Then he looked at Kevin. "Kevin, if you are interested in joining the G-Men when you turn eighteen, here is my card with my contact information."

Cadmus pulled a card out of his front pocket and handed it to Shade, who then put it between the cushions on the couch. The card sank into the shadows between the seat cushions and then fell from the ceiling into my hands. I glanced at the card, which read thus:

CADMUS SMITH
DIRECTOR OF DEPARTMENT OF SUPERPOWERED AND
EXTRATERRESTRIAL BEINGS
This was followed by his phone number and email, along with

the address of his office.

Then I heard movement and looked up to see that Cadmus and Shade standing up. Cadmus nodded one last time at Dad, who only glared at him, before walking toward the door. I stepped out of their way, allowing Cadmus—who didn't look at me—to pass. Shade also passed, but unlike Cadmus, she winked at me, which took me by surprise, so I didn't know how to react until they were both out the door and gone.

A moment later, I heard the doors of their van open and close. Then I saw, through the door window, the van drive down the street away from our house.

Turning to face my parents, I said, "What was that?"

"Another government scam," said Dad, who sounded just as angry as ever. "Don't take it seriously. The G-Men are always trying to lure young neoheroes like you into their service, but you can't trust them."

I nodded slowly. "Uh, right. Well, I guess I'll just be going to my room, then. Is dinner ready yet, Mom?"

Mom shook her head. She looked a little shaken by the appearance of Cadmus and Shade, even though neither of them had behaved threateningly. "Not yet, but it will be within the next ten minutes. I need to go back to the kitchen and make sure that the sauce is coming along."

Mom stood up and walked into the kitchen, while I walked down the hall to my room, but not before I glanced over my shoulder and saw Dad still sitting in his recliner. He was scowling fiercely, like he was reliving some bad memories that he didn't want to remember. I had no idea what Dad's history with Cadmus or the G-Men was, but I decided that now was probably not the time to ask.

When I shut the door to my room, I sat down on my bed and looked at the card with Cadmus Smith's contact information on it. I wasn't really interested in joining the G-Men, mostly because I figured that if Dad distrusted them, then so should I. Still, Cadmus Smith was an important person, so I figured it would be useful to have his contact information on hand. So I slipped the card into my backpack so I wouldn't lose it.

Then I placed my backpack on the floor and started to get ready for dinner. As I took off my shoes and socks, I thought about the future. I didn't know what the future held for me and my family or how the G-Men or the NHA would play into it, but I knew, beyond a shadow of a doubt, that this was not going to be my last adventure as Bolt.

-

The story continues in *The Superhero's Team*, now available wherever books are sold!

About the Author

Lucas Flint writes superhero fiction. He is the author of The Superhero's Son, Minimum Wage Sidekick, The Legacy Superhero, and Capes Online, among others.

Find links to books, social media, updates on newest releases, and more by going to his website at www.lucasflint.com.

Or just use your phone to scan the QR code below to go to my website instead:

Made in United States
North Haven, CT
21 March 2022